LAKE OF FURY

Talos Cord was the second man from UN Field Reconnaissance to go to the East African republic of Moyalla. His predecessor, who had been investigating arms-smuggling, had been killed in a plane crash which looked like sabotage. But had the plane been sabotaged because another of the passengers was the son of the virtual ruler of the Lake Calu district? Even when Talos Cord found the truth, it was a gamble whether he could do much about it.

BILL KNOX

---◆---

LAKE OF FURY

Complete and Unabridged

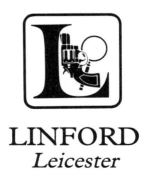

LINFORD
Leicester

First published in Great Britain
as 'Lake of Fury' by
Robert MacLeod

First Linford Edition
published 1996

British Library CIP Data

Knox, Bill, *1928* –
Lake of fury.—Large print ed.—
Linford mystery library
1. English fiction—20th century
I. Title
823.9'14 [F]

ISBN 0–7089–7932–7

Published by
F. A. Thorpe (Publishing) Ltd.
Anstey, Leicestershire
Set by Words & Graphics Ltd.
Anstey, Leicestershire
Printed and bound in Great Britain by
T. J. Press (Padstow) Ltd., Padstow, Cornwall

This book is printed on acid-free paper

For
Sheila and Harvey

1

WHEN they'd flown down the coast the sea had been that rich electric blue which seems exclusive to the vast basin where the Indian Ocean meets the East African continental shelf. But then the little plane had swung west, inland, for long, throbbing miles over the arid bushland — and now they'd come to this great dulled mirror of an inland lake, lifeless and grey despite the blazing sunlight.

"Down there, m'sieu." The pilot, a round-faced young Frenchman named Duvert, nudged his passenger in the ribs. "That is where it happened."

Talos Cord's face stayed expressionless as the small blue Marchetti with the white United Nations badges suddenly banked and swooped towards the lake. He could see for himself. Down there, where it had lain for more than a week,

1

the shape of the crashed transport plane shimmered up from beneath the water like a broken silver cross.

Twenty-six men had died in the plane, an old D.C.3 run by a shoestring airline. One of these men was the reason why he'd been sent to Lake Calu.

"Thanks." He gave a faint nod and sat silent as Duvert, vaguely annoyed at his passenger's apparent lack of interest, levelled the Marchetti. It's single-engined shadow swept on across the lake's surface, low enough for its two occupants to see the patchwork of cultivated fields along its shore and here and there the stakes of a native fishing trap protruding from its shallows.

Cord sighed to himself. It was only four hours since he'd landed at Nygall, capital of the republic of Moyalla, aboard a scheduled B.O.A.C. jet from Rome. Armed soldiers and sandbagged machine gun posts at the airport had been a reminder that the country's northern territory was in an ugly mood and that the latest regime had more than its share of troubles. That didn't concern him. His task lay in the south, where things were peacefully pro-government — a point stressed by the U.N. agencies director for Moyalla in the quick, private meeting they'd had at the airport before Cord had been passed on to Paul Duvert's aerial taxi.

Life had its ups and downs. Back in Rome, Cord had been faced with the happy prospect of a job newly completed, a month's back pay in his pocket, and a blossoming friendship with a petite brunette. Now, instead, there was this.

A twist of a grin crossed his face and puckered to a halt against the long curve of the hairline scar on his left cheek. The money, at any rate, would be waiting when he was finished.

Duvert nudged him again and gestured towards the seat belt.

Cord obeyed. When he'd finished fastening the harness and looked up they were coming in to land. A hitherto unseen huddle of buildings sat close by the water's edge and a long strip of glinting wire-mesh runway waited their arrival.

Moments later, the Marchetti's tricycle undercarriage touched down with a bump and a lurch. As they slowed, Duvert's fingers moved lightly over the controls, the engine roared again, and they swung off the strip in a rising fog of yellow dust. The little plane jolted rapidly towards a tin-roofed hut where a faded yellow windsock hung limp from an old pole.

"El Wabir," announced Duvert, his voice raised above the engine's bellow. The aircraft came to a halt, he cut the power, and the propeller died with a whine. "Not what the sane man would call a metropolis — but at least they have a refrigerator for the beer."

"Which helps," agreed Cord with suitable solemnity. The dust haze was settling, and he had a chance to look around.

There wasn't much. Another aircraft,

a modern twin-engined executive Dove finished in gleaming red and silver, was parked about fifty yards away. Further away, a solitary truck sat beside a modest storeshed. Over by the tin-roofed hut with its woebegone windsock were a battered Volkswagen and a dust-covered late-model Pontiac coupe. The only sign of life was at the hut's doorway, where a thin, coffee-skinned Moyallan in ragged shorts and an old singlet squatted in the shade.

"Were you to be met, M'sieu Cord?" queried Duvert with a determined curiosity. He prided himself in knowing most things about his passengers. But all he'd gleaned from this one in almost four hundred and fifty miles was that he had business with the Lake Calu agent of the Food and Agricultural Organisation — not that there was anything else likely to bring a U.N. man to El Wabir.

"Uh-huh." At ground level and under that high, baleful sun, the temperature was already soaring within the perspex dome of the cockpit's canopy. Cord unclipped his harness and collected his single suitcase from the spare seat behind them. "By a man called Spence — know him?"

"But of course." Duvert permitted himself a chuckle at the name. "John Spence is known to everyone who stops at El Wabir. But — well, he is not always punctual with his arrangements."

"It looks that way," murmured Cord wryly. It fitted, too, with what he'd been told of the local F.A.O. agent's somewhat erratic temperament. He slid open the passenger door, shifted his grip on the suitcase, and glanced expectantly at the pilot. "Coming?"

While the man was still freeing himself from his harness Cord swung down from the plane to the dry, gritty earth, and treated himself to the luxury of an uninhibited, animal-like stretch of every muscle. He could feel the perspiration already gathering between his shoulderblades and the very air he breathed brought a new dryness to his throat and lungs. But at least he'd arrived. He stretched again and gave a grunt of pleasure.

Coming round from his side of the Marchetti, Duvert raised an eyebrow at the sight then shrugged. A strange but interesting one, this passenger named Cord, he decided. The phrase might be 'well put together' — just over medium height, slim and muscular beneath that lightweight brown jacket worn over an open-necked fawn shirt, with khaki twill slacks and soft, well-worn moccasins.

Usually the face was what mattered. Talos Cord was clean-shaven, his black hair cut short. Dark, slightly tired eyes sat above a strong nose and a wide, easy-going mouth. It was a face bronzed by wind as well as sun — and then there was that scar. It should have made the rest coarse . . . *mais au contraire*, instead it contributed a strangely purposeful air of ability.

As they set off towards the airstrip

office, Cord thumbed towards the other aircraft. "Another visitor?"

"Not that one." Duvert gave a slightly envious scowl. "It belongs to Lucas Darrald, like most things around here. Still — " he shrugged with momentary pity — "his son was on that plane in the lake."

And, apart from the pilot and co-pilot, had been the only European aboard, Cord could have added. The name had been at the top of the list — Frank Darrald, aged twenty-six, missing presumed drowned, body not yet recovered.

"If he'd used the Dove — "

"He was not a pilot," said Duvert briefly. He changed the subject. "This airstrip, of course, is neither Mr Darrald's nor our own. It belongs to the oil company working over on the north-west."

They'd reached the low wooden steps leading to the hut. The native squatting in the shade rolled the cigarette between his lips to one corner of his mouth

8

and showed his teeth in a perfunctory greeting. Duvert marched past him, beckoning Cord to follow.

The interior of the airstrip's office had the same neglected air. Even the magazine pin-ups on the walls seemed faded and forlorn. Furniture was restricted to a desk, a couple of filing cabinets, a rusted, white-fronted refrigerator and a row of empty coathooks. Two men sat on rickety chairs beside the desk, and Duvert greeted them with a nod.

The older of the two, a faded, sun-dried European with a two-day stubble of beard, rose to his feet.

"Mr Cord?" he queried briefly. "For John Spence?"

Cord nodded.

"I'm Johann Balder, airfield manager." He sniffed, turned wearily towards the refrigerator, opened it, extracted two bottles of beer, and knocked the caps off with a practised skill. He thumped the bottles in front of them. "Compliments of Mid-Con Petroleum."

"The welcoming ritual," said the other man with an acid touch of amusement. He was a tall muscular African dressed in immaculately clean shirt and slacks, the voice was almost accent free, studied in its laziness, and his eyes held a bright curiosity. "*Salaam*, Mr Cord — and what do you think of El Wabir?"

Cord took a long drink from the bottle before he answered. The golden liquid was no masterpiece of brewing but it was cool and wet and infinitely thirst-quenching.

"The public relations side works well," he said with a grin of contentment.

The Moyallan approved. "Richard Nyeme," he introduced himself, staying where he was. "How was the flight?"

Duvert answered, his own drink considerably diminished. "No problems, light west wind, some cloud forecast near the coast. Going out?"

Nyeme nodded. "Mr Darrald has business," he said briefly. Then, for Cord's benefit, he explained, "I am

10

his pilot, among other things." His face had the fine, almost Arab features of the coast Moyallans, his skin was a light coffee colour, and the wrist watch he wore was gold with a heavy matching bracelet.

"John Spence looked in this morning and said you'd be arriving," said Balder, leaning against the refrigerator as if guarding its contents. "He's some calls to make — and if he wasn't back on time he'd meet you in the village."

"Where?"

"Our place." Balder scratched his stubble. "Mid-Con have their district office in El Wabir. But there's no hurry."

For some reason, Duvert grinned. Nyeme contented himself with a grunt, then glanced again towards Cord.

"Your first visit to our part of Moyalla, Mr Cord?"

Cord nodded. "A kind of fact-finding trip," he said vaguely. "We're interested in a possible expansion of local development."

"Good." The African nodded wisely. "Our country needs that kind of help — and your U.N. people earn respect."

"But not much more," growled Duvert half under his breath. He turned towards Balder. "Johann, kick that lazy black devil off your front step and tell him I want the Marchetti refuelled." He scowled. "This time, I'll watch him myself."

"Wani's all right — " began Balder uneasily.

"He is not," said Nyeme softly. "He is a lazy black devil, like Duvert said. But then, colour apart, he is not alone, is he?"

Balder flushed, shrugged and then, his mouth a tight line, headed for the door. His voice sounded outside.

"*Mtundu* . . . the fool." Nyeme laughed but with scant humour. "Such men annoy me. A petty little man with a petty little job."

Embarrassed, Duvert cleared his throat. "Perhaps you would like me to walk with you to the village, M'sieu Cord?"

"Just point me in the right direction and I'll manage," Cord assured him. He picked up his suitcase, raised his other hand in a brief farewell to Nyeme, and followed the Frenchman to the door.

Outside, the verandah steps were deserted. Duvert led him a few paces beyond the hut then pointed towards the straggling outskirts of the village, separated from the airstrip by a few hundred yards to tall, coarse *ban* grass.

"There is a track a little way down," he directed. "Follow it, and it will take you straight into the market-place, such as that is. From there you will see a tree, the only one in the place and a miserable specimen. Behind it is the oil company's office, with a sign above the door." He gave a sly, sideways grin. "You will find a surprise there, my friend."

"What kind?"

The grin became a wink, but the man wouldn't elaborate. "And now I

13

must go too, to watch this refuelling," he declared. "I have two boxes on the plane, vaccines for the medical centre over at Laicha. That means a two hour flight from here."

They shook hands and parted.

The track was easy enough to find, a tyre-rutted path which seemed to hold more than its fair quota of insect life. Cord trudged along and swore softly as he brushed a minor swarm of flies from around his forehead. He stopped took one of the fat, dark brown cheroots he carried in his jacket's handkerchief pocket, lit it, and puffed the smoke in a determined self-defence. With a sigh he picked up the suitcase and walked on.

Far away, in the air-conditioned comfort of an office in in the slab-sided U.N. Secretariat Headquarters at New York, he was just a pin that had been moved to a new location on the world map. Field Reconnaissance Section moved their pins all the time — while Andrew Beck, the fat, untidy Section chief, sat and fumed into one or other of his three desk telephones.

Field Reconnaissance specialised in looking for international troubles before they came to the boil, then advising on the best way to make things cool down — when it didn't in fact take steps in that direction on its own. A sensitive ear for the earliest murmurs, for apparently unrelated rumour was Andrew Beck's chief stock in trade. His remedy was to drop one of his men into the situation like a blob of phosphorus then wait for results.

This time the system hadn't worked — or perhaps it had, though not in a way even Beck would have wished.

The message to Talos Cord had been brief, brutal, yet filled with its own cold mixture of unspoken loss and bitter anger.

'TOLLOGO, LAST REPORT FILED TANZANIA, KILLED PLANE CRASH LAKE CALU, MOYALLA. INVESTIGATE AND EXPEDITE. BRIEFING DESPATCHED.'

Robert Tollogo, aged twenty-eight, Sudanese, four years service with Field Reconnaissance, had been found after a three month silence. Found because a body with two fingers missing from the left hand and with tribal markings on its broad chest had drifted ashore.

The briefing waiting at Nygall Airport had told the rest. Beck had given Tollogo the job of finding out more about whispers concerning a growing cash-and-carry supply of modern weapons to any rebel African faction with money to spend, stories which weren't just the usual scandals of Government surplus rifles or out-dated ammunition.

Mortars, anti-tank guns, rockets — even, it was suggested, aircraft — could be got if the price was paid. A slender lead had brought Robert Tollogo from Mozambique to Tanzania. His next report had hinted cautiously at something even bigger than the whispers had admitted.

And now he was dead . . . yet,

strangely, Moyalla was one of the few countries where the organisation seemed to have made no attempt to contact its potential clients. That could mean the faction in the northern territory had no cash to spare — or, just possibly, that the organisation didn't want to encourage trouble in the country for reasons of their own.

A thin, wary-eyed dog growled briefly from the edge of the grass, where it crouched over some unidentifiable plunder. Cord shrugged almost sympathetically in its direction, then walked the rest of the way into the village.

Like most of its kind El Wabir was a mixture of African traditional and European discard. Bell-shaped thatches and clay-brick walls crowded beside ramshackle structures of corrugated iron and packing case wood. An assortment of near-naked young *mtotos* played noisily around the carefully sanded doorways, stopping briefly to inspect him as he passed.

Their elders, going about their

business, showed scant interest. Strange Europeans who carried their own suitcases from the airstrip were of little importance that much they'd learned in the time since the oil company had first descended on their village.

He found the market place without trouble. A gaudily painted beer hall and a Sikh trader's open-fronted shop were flanked by a double handful of small, makeshift stalls which smelled mainly of fish and rancid fat. They were busy with customers — most in a mixture of cast-off European dress, but a few still in the long, tube-like robes of the country. One of them, a tall aloof tribesman from the far-out bush, had an ancient long-barrelled Martini rifle slung over his shoulder as he listened to the tinny note of a cheap transistor radio.

Cord chuckled, then looked around. Duvert's tree, a gnarled, thick-waisted cedar, guided him on to the Mid-Con office, a two storey frame building painted white.

A shop-type bell clanged as he pushed open the door and went in. It shut behind him, and he found himself at a narrow counter running across an outer office. A fan whirred overhead, churning a semblance of coolness into the air.

"*Jambo, bwana.*" The grey-haired Moyallan woman who came through from the curtained door at the rear smiled a greeting and hitched at the waist of her brightly patterned cotton skirt. "You look for Miss Jean?"

"I — " Cord hesitated, dredging together the few scraps of Swahili he possessed. "My name is Cord. For Bwana Spence. *Umeelewa* . . . you understand?"

She grinned, showing a broken assortment of teeth. "*Ndio.* For Miss Jean." She disappeared into the inner office.

Cord sighed, ground out the stub of his cheroot on the counter ashtray, and waited.

The woman reappeared again,

beamed, opened the counter flap, and beckoned him through. He followed her, past the curtained doorway and along a narrow hallway. She squeezed to one side and waved him into the first of the rooms.

It was another, smaller office. There was a girl standing in front of its single desk — a girl which made him understand Duvert's winking promise of 'a surprise'. She was medium height, a few pounds short of being plump, with a freckled, golden-brown complexion and rich chestnut hair.

"You're earlier than John Spence expected, Mr Cord." The voice was crisply friendly. Grey eyes which held a fleck of green inspected him with casual interest. "How was your trip?"

"Smooth enough." She was, he reckoned, about twenty-six. She wore her hair long, so that it brushed the neck of her olive green shirt-blouse as she crossed towards him. Fine, unbleached cotton slacks were held at her waist by a broad belt of tanned leather. She had firm, small breasts, and her face, with its broad cheekbones and a wide, determined mouth, softened as she smiled.

"I'm Jean Berry — my brother and I staff this outpost of the oil empire." She cocked her head a little to one side. "I could offer you a seat and a drink, but I've a feeling you'd prefer a chance to freshen up."

He grinned. "Does it show that much?"

She laughed in return. "No, but I believe in first things first. Leave your case — you want the second door along."

The bathroom was tiled in a pink plastic, the towels were fresh and lightly scented, and the shelf above the basin held a new cake of soap, still in its wrappings. By the time he'd washed away the worst of the travel grime Cord had come round to deciding that El Wabir might be more promising than it had seemed.

Jean Berry was back behind the desk

when he returned to her office. She looked up and nodded approvingly. "You look better, at any rate."

"And feel it," he agreed, taking the chair she indicated. "When do you expect Spence to arrive?"

"Soon, I hope." She shrugged with a mild amusement. "You can never be sure when he goes off on his rounds. But he's corning back here all right — we act as his unofficial message centre."

Cord decided against a cheroot, produced his cigarettes, and offered them across the desk. She took one, accepted a light, then grimaced apologetically. "I said something about a drink, didn't I?"

"There was beer at the airstrip," said Cord.

"There's always beer at the airstrip." Her voice held the same mild amusement. "Standard welcome for travellers — and at least it gives Johann something to do." She leaned back in her chair as the native woman reappeared in the doorway. "I usually eat about now, and Zeneb always cooks enough for two. Like to join me?"

"I thought of trying to find somewhere — "

"There's only the local guesthouse," she said dryly. "I wouldn't let my worst enemy eat there."

"*Ahasante*, Zeneb. In five minutes." As the woman went out, Jean Berry turned her attention back to her visitor. "Exactly what is this Field Reconnaissance section you're with, Mr Cord? I've heard most of your U.N. labels, but it's a new one. Even John didn't seem sure — and that rather upset him." She grimaced. "He's got an idea you're some sort of travelling inspector, liable to haul him over the coals for overstepping his budget."

Cord stubbed his cigarette in the big gourd shell placed near his elbow. "We look around and size up prospects," he said vaguely. "Sometimes we're in fresh territory, sometimes where there's already some kind of programme. Then we make recommendations. But Spence needn't worry. He might even end up being happy I've come."

"Development survey stuff." The grey eyes watched him for a moment then flicked briefly away. "We've plenty of that in the oil business."

He eased away from the subject. "Maybe your brother could help me."

"Hal?" She nodded. "He knows a fair amount about the area — we've been here a couple of years. You could ask him tomorrow night, when the land train comes back." She saw the blank look on his face. "That's what we call it, anyway. It's a big tractor-trailer unit for cross-country haulage." Her left hand waved vaguely across the room. "This is really a glorified freight office, nothing more."

"For what kind of operation?" The briefing he'd received had, as usual, been skeleton in outline. Andrew Beck liked his men to fill in their own detail.

The girl used a pencil to scratch

lightly behind one ear. "Well, at the start Mid-Con moved into Moyalla on a crazy notion there might be oil around Lake Calu. That's when the airstrip was built. The idea fizzled out, but then they hit natural gas about a hundred miles north-west of here, practically in the middle of nowhere. They're carrying out a series of test bores to see if it's big enough to be a commercial proposition — they'd need to pipe it over into Kenya or right across to the coast, and that could cost plenty."

Several hundred miles of pipeline would amount to a major operation, even for a giant oil combine. "And the land train?"

"I'll show you." She got up, and Cord followed her through to the outer office. A map was pinned across one end of the counter top, covered by a square of plastic sheeting.

"We're here." The girl pointed to the blue which marked Lake Cain. "There's a fairly good road all the way from the coast, so Mid-Con can truck in supplies and equipment this far. Then Hal's land train moves the stuff out to the drilling area." Her finger swept across the plastic. "They're working in this area, a mixture of swamp and bush. Getting there and back takes him about three days."

"I see." He concentrated on the map. "Where's the Darrald estate located?"

"The *Tillik Sau*'s place?" She waved aside a fly which had been coming in to land. "That's what the Moyallans call him, the Big Boss."

"Makes his money from chemicals and timber," murmured Cord. "I'm hoping to meet him."

"It may not be the best of times." She glanced sideways at him. "You know about his son?"

He nodded. "Unfortunate, but I've a job to do."

"That's your problem." Her voice cooled a little. "If you have to see him, he lives at what they call 'the farm' — about twenty miles west of here, where the hills begin. There's a reasonable road. He owns — " she frowned at the map, then drew a rough circle over a plate-sized area of its surface — "all of that, maybe more."

"Quite an empire," agreed Cord. "I met one of his men at the airstrip, waiting to fly him out on some business trip."

"Richarn Nyeme?" She turned away from the map and leaned back against the counter. "He's one good example of what education can do for a bush *mtoto*. Lucas Darrald is supposed to have paid his way through college. Flying aeroplanes is a part-time occupation for Richarn — he's a qualified accountant."

"A handy character to have around." Cord rubbed his chin. "But I'd imagine Darrald maybe doesn't feel the same about air travel after what's happened."

"The *Tillik Sau* is made of pretty tough material — even though Frank meant a lot to him."

"An only son?"

She nodded. "Yes. But — well, at least he didn't see the plane go down. I did." She winced a little at the memory. "One minute it was climbing over the lake the next it just fell out of the sky."

While the men in that metal shell had a last few moments to realise they were going to die. Cord's mouth tightened. "Has Darrald any other family?"

"His wife died a few years back, but there's a daughter, Paula. She's been away from home lately." Jean Berry seemed to feel they'd talked enough. "Let's find out about lunch. Zeneb doesn't like being kept waiting."

★ ★ ★

They ate in an upstairs room, gay with chintz curtains, deep leather armchairs and a tall native vase filled with a burst of mimosa blossom. Slatted window blinds shaded them from the glare of the outside world. The meal was simple

28

but appetising, beginning with melon, then a main course of antelope steak. Finally, while Zeneb cleared up, Jean Berry produced an earthenware pot of pungent black local coffee.

By the time she'd poured him a second cup he knew a little more about this girl with the chestnut hair. Brother and sister had worked for Mid-Con on postings to many countries. For them, two years in Moyalla was almost a record length of stay.

"You travel around too, Mr Cord — "

"Make it Talos," he suggested.

"All right." She relaxed in her chair. "Anyway, most U.N. people get around. How did it start with you?"

"You could say I hadn't much to do with it. It just happened." Almost unconsciously, his hand strayed to the scar on his cheek. Even now, after all these years, it was a story he fought shy of telling — fought shy without really being sure why he felt that way.

It was close on three o'clock when

John Spence finally arrived to collect him. In his late forties, bald with a fluffy tonsure-like fringe, tall and conscious enough of it to walk with a slight stoop, he was a thin-faced, rather weary-eyed figure. He greeted Cord warily, then smiled more readily towards Jean.

"I'm sorry I'm late," he told her apologetically in a mild but unmistakable Scots accent.

"I'd a feeling you might be held back," said Jean with a friendly sarcasm. "Have you eaten yet, John?"

The F.A.O. agent nodded. "Dhurra cakes and an unidentifiable stew at my last call but one — token of thanks for services rendered."

"Another satisfied customer?" queried Cord.

Spence eyed him suspiciously. "There's both satisfied and dissatisfied around here, Mr Cord. This was a fellow whose cows had milk fever. Not so long ago he'd have blamed witchcraft, but now he knows there's a magic called antibiotics."

"You're kept pretty busy."

"Aye." Spence nodded brusquely. "You'll find out for yourself, I hope. That's what you're here for, isn't it?"

"Among other things."

Spence shrugged and turned away. "Jean, I gave Zeneb a couple of chickens I collected — they're more use to you than me. And thanks for this favour." His mouth tightened, awkwardly. "If there are no messages — "

"None," she assured him.

"Then we'll be on our way. I've other calls to make." A bitter edge entered his voice. "It'll give Mr Cord here a start to his studies."

They said goodbye and left. Spence had a much-worn Ford utility parked outside the company office, painted pale blue, a home-made truck platform tacked on behind the front cab. Once his passenger and the suitcase were aboard, the Scot jabbed the engine to life, grated the utility into gear, and set off in a stubbornly determined fashion.

"She's a nice girl," said Cord conversationally.

"Aye." Spence horn-blasted a group of natives from his path. They grinned and waved as they recognised the Ford and its driver. He grunted, and raised one hand from the wheel in a vague salute. "A lot better than her brother." Then, as if he'd used up his quota of words, his mouth shut tight.

They were clear of the village, heading along a track parallel with Lake Calu, before he spoke again. "I didn't get much warning you were coming."

"They didn't exactly give me a month's notice," countered Cord. "Who's first on your list this afternoon?"

The tall figure hunched a little more over the steering wheel. "A local headman named Kalloe — more advanced than most around here. I've been getting him to try planting an Egyptian strain of cotton seed — the local variety is low-yield stuff."

There were flamingoes down by the

lake, scores of wading pink and white shapes, feeding in the shallows. Cord watched them ruefully. In one sense it did no harm for Spence to regard him as an unnecessary intruder. For now, a minor feud between them would help establish his cover story. Later perhaps . . . he dragged a cheroot from his top pocket, struck a match, and smoked in silence.

They turned off the track a little way on, and a few hundred yards of lurching low-gear travel brought them to a quartet of native huts set close together at the edge of a parcel of cultivated fields. Spence halted the Ford beside the largest of the huts, switched off the engine, and Cord followed him out. A goat was tethered nearby, the inevitable dog was already barking, but the huts were deserted.

"They're all at work, but they'll have seen us," said Spence briefly. "Let's get on with it."

They'd unloaded half a dozen medium-sized sacks from the rear of the utility by the time the headman arrived from the fields. Kalloe was a muscular, surprisingly young man with a proud face and a glistening, sweat-stained body. His feet were bare and dust-covered, he wore a pair of crumpled, ragged shorts, and his eyes narrowed a little at the sight of a stranger.

"*Jambo*." Spence strode forward, spoke to the man in a low voice for a moment, and received a vigorous nod in reply. Kalloe's face brightened, he wiped one hand on the side of his shorts, and extended it as he crossed over.

"*Ahasante*." He shook hands in pumping, enthusiastic fashion.

"I told him you've come from the capital because you've heard how the men at Lake Calu are bringing new life to their soil," muttered Spence in slight embarrassment. "It does no harm, and he deserves some encouragement."

"Tell him I'm happy to be here," said Cord softly. "And put it any way you want."

Spence looked at him for a moment, then seemed to thaw a little. "Aye, I'll do that."

The seed was handed over, Kalloe signed a receipt in laborious, mission-school printing, and they were on their way again after another formal handshaking.

"He's happy anyway," mused Cord as the utility regained the main track.

"It would help if they were all like that one," said Spence, wincing a little as they hit a pothole deeper than the rest. "He should do all right wi' that cotton. The local stuff's the yellow flower variety — you know what that means."

Cord nodded, keeping what he hoped was a look of interest on his face.

The F.A.O. agent's 'other calls' stretched into a weary list of seven, spread over endless, dusty miles. One was a herdsman who wanted someone to kill a wandering leopard which was prowling too near his cattle at night. Another was a worried ancient who

35

declared that his wife had run off taking his best plough-blade along with her. In between there was a sick cow, a cheerful villain who claimed that baboons had raided his stock of corn seed, and an earnest discussion on why a set of lakeside fish traps were wrongly placed.

At last, Spence turned the Ford back towards El Wabir.

"Well?" he demanded wearily.

"You've got to be a little bit of everything," mused Cord. Even as a spectator he'd found it a gruelling few hours.

"Aye." Spence scowled and his foot pressed harder on the accelerator. "But I know how minds work back at Headquarters." He waved briefly as they passed another vehicle, an old truck with a native driver perched behind the wheel. "Most of these people have to be taught from the ground up. It takes time — a lot of it."

"You could use some help," suggested Cord.

"I manage." He seemed ready to say more, then thought better of it.

It was almost dusk when they arrived at the F.A.O. agent's base, located on a small rise of ground a couple of miles from El Wabir. Two sectional aluminum huts and a larger living unit sat side by side within a neat compound surrounded by a low hedge of planted thornbush.

Spence drew the Ford to a shuddering halt, climbed out stiffly, and led the way into his home. The main room was simply furnished with a table and chairs, a small roll-top desk and a few book cases contrived from packing cases. The floor was bare, polished wood and a compact two-way radio unit stood in one corner.

"Like a drink?" Spence didn't wait for an answer but crossed to the desk, unlocked it, and produced a half-full bottle of whisky.

"Thanks." Cord watched the Scot find two glasses in another drawer. Two generous measures gurgled from the bottle and he was handed one.

"Here's to whatever you're doing, Mr Cord," said Spence dryly. He took a long gulp of the liquor and sighed.

Cord followed his example. The neat whisky burned down towards his stomach, and spread its welcome glow.

"There's nothing like a wee refreshment at the end of the day." Spence firmly re-corked the bottle, put it back in its pigeon-hole, and locked the desk again. The key went into his pocket. "Eh — use the transceiver any time you want. The wavelength and call-sign stuff are posted on a card somewhere. If you prefer the telephone, the nearest is in El Wabir — when the line works. I make a daily 8 a.m. call from here to Nygall, and that's enough as far as I'm concerned."

A polite cough sounded from the doorway and a plump, middle-aged Moyallan in a white jacket and over-long shorts moved quietly into the shadowed room.

"This is Sildo, a daft devil sent to plague me," declared Spence, his thin features relaxing in an approach to a grin. The houseboy nodded solemnly towards their guest. "He understands a damned sight more than he lets on."

The Moyallan kept the same solemn expression. "If you come, *bwana*, a room is ready," he declared in slow, stilted English. He crossed over, picked up Cord's suitcase, and glanced briefly towards his employer. "And if the Bwana Spence had returned when he promised, the meal that is waiting would not be burned."

Spence gave a groan of despair.

★ ★ ★

The room he'd been given was small, with an army type cot bed and a plain wooden dressing table. A diesel generator throbbed somewhere outside in the grey dusk, and a single overhead bulb blazed down from the ceiling. A basin of water and a clean towel had been laid out on an iron stand.

Once the houseboy had gone Cord sprawled back on the bed and stared thoughtfully at the ceiling. So far, he'd done little except go through the motions of being a Food and Agriculture man from some obscure section on an equally obscure mission.

What he needed now was a hard starting point.

The airstrip office? He nodded to himself. Robert Tollogo had been only one of the people in that transport plane, but that still didn't mean his death had been accidental.

Half an hour later, washed, wearing a clean shirt from his case, he was summoned through to join Spence.

The table was set, they took their places, and ate in silence. Whatever Sildo's threats, the meal, of chicken stew with rice and wild onions, was only a little crisp round the edges.

Spence pushed back his chair. "Fancy a turn outside?" he asked. Cord nodded and followed him out into

40

the compound yard. They walked along the thorn hedge's boundary, the diesel generator purring steadily in the background, the moon above a yellowed ball which cast strange shadows around them.

"You'll want transport and a guide for this survey nonsense, I suppose," said Spence suddenly. "You'll understand I'd do it myself but — "

"But you've enough on your plate," Cord finished it for him. "It would help — I'll probably be around for a few days."

"Hmmph." Spence produced an old cherrywood pipe from his pocket, removed the scrap of paper which had held the tobacco in the bowl, and struck a match. He puffed for a moment. "I've a jeep you can borrow . . . it usually keeps running. I'll see what can be done about the guide. David Saat may be able to help there."

"Who's he?"

"The local police inspector. He's fairly friendly."

"He sounds a good bet," agreed Cord. "How is law and order around here?"

Spence shrugged. "We've none of the troubles of the northern area, if that's what you mean. Things are reasonable, apart from the odd bunch of *shifta* bandits wandering in from across the border. They've never bothered me — well, except once."

"When did it happen?"

The Scot yawned a little. "Not long back — a few nights before the plane crash."

Talos Cord felt a sudden chill of misgiving. "What happened?"

"Not much," confessed Spence. "It was a queer business, though. They raided the compound while I was out on call and Sildo was down at the village — turned the place upside down as if they were looking for something. Maybe they'd fallen for that old story that every U.N. agent has a bag of gold hidden under his bed."

"Did they take anything?" Cord

fought the bitter understanding from his voice.

"Nothing, and that was the queer part of it." Spence sighed. "It's a bit of an insult in its own way. They just made one devil of a mess, and left me needing a new lock on my desk."

"You told the police?"

"Yes. But they didn't get anywhere." The man yawned, more openly. "Well, I've got an early start in the morning . . . "

Cord nodded. "I'll stay out for a spell."

"Suit yourself . . . goodnight, then." John Spence knocked the last of the ash from his pipe, and headed back towards the house.

Somewhere out in the bush a hyena gave a long, hysterical laugh. Cord's mouth tightened at the sound.

A *shifta* raid in which nothing was taken. It was all the proof he needed that Robert Tollogo's cover had been broken, that the men he'd been up against had had a vague knowledge

43

that there was a link between Tollogo and some U.N. agency.

The hyena laughed again and another, more distant, answered. Talos Cord swore softly to himself and turned away.

2

A SHAFT of pale moonlight cut across the darkened room and carved its shape on the blank wall opposite the window. Talos Cord lay on the cover of the cot bed, hands behind his head, letting the time pass with an acquired patience. Close on two hours had passed since he'd first entered the little cubicle and settled down to wait. First there had been the clatter of dishes and pad of feet as Silda, the houseboy, cleared up for the night. Then it had ended and a little later the diesel generator had switched off.

Now all that remained were the sounds of the night world outside his window. On the moonlit wall, a tiny house-lizard patterned its way up towards the dark shadow of ceiling in effortless, scampering style. He smiled at the sight, remembering another lizard in another place.

That one had been a bewildered small boy's friend and companion in a constant background of waiting — the vague half-life of a civilian internment camp at Shanghai. He'd been eight years old when the Japs finally surrendered.

One hand went up to his face to touch the long scar on his cheek. It had been an open, crusted wound when a Jap sergeant had first handed him in at the camp gate, handed him in to be cared for by a strangely understanding White Russian ex-colonel and one-time Eurasian taxi-dancer. He could remember nothing of life before that camp. His name? 'P. Cord' was printed on the tag sewn into the neckband of the ragged shirt he'd worn.

When it was all over, an officer called Andrew Beck had been one of the first Allied soldiers to arrive. Beck had taken the boy under his wing, worked on that shirt tag, traced it back to a shipload of civilians sunk while trying to escape from Hong Kong.

Peter Cord, orphan, unclaimed — Beck had taken him, rechristened him 'Talos', explained it, made the story as important a nightly ritual as cleaning teeth or sleeping in a bed which had soft linen sheets.

Outside, somewhere in the bush, an animal screamed and died and the victor gave a brief, coughing roar. Cord winced, fumbled in his shirt pocket for a cheroot and chewed it gently, unlit.

He could still hear Andrew Beck tell that story in his soft, deep growl. The Cretan legend of how King Minos had possessed a giant bronze robot named Talos, a robot powered by a magic fluid. It had patrolled the shores of the old island kingdom, untiringly faithful, incorruptibly reliable, a defence against invaders, an enforcer of law. Until, at last, a woman named Medea had pulled a drainplug from its heel and the magic fluid had run from its body.

Maybe Beck had a moral there too.

But above all he'd been looking to a time ahead, creating his own Talos, a man whose loyalty was to the world, whose family tree was an ideal. Only one factor had occasionally intervened. Cord was no robot but healthily human.

He was never sure whether Andrew Beck regretted it or not.

It was close on midnight when he finally rose from the cot bed, slipped on his jacket, and took the pen-sized torch and combination folding knife from his suitcase. The knife was Swedish, with a surprising variety of blades packed within its fat bone handle. As he lifted it out his fingers touched the small metal box which lay beneath. Inside, nestling in oilskin, was a Neuhausen automatic and its clips of black, glistening 9 mm Parabellum cartridges. He shook his head, left the box, and put the other two items in his pocket.

Two minutes later he was outside the house, standing beneath John Spence's bedroom window, hearing the

F.A.O. man's steady, rasping snore. He grinned, and moved quietly across the compound towards the shadow-strewn bushland.

★ ★ ★

The wind murmured through the *ban* grass and the blacker thorn patches, small unseen creatures rustled away from Cord's path as he headed for the airstrip. He used the stars as his compass on a wide, curving course which kept well clear of El Wabir. Any East African village had its quota of prowling, half-wild dogs, instinctively antagonistic to strangers in the night — and he'd no wish to meet up with them.

It was half an hour past midnight when he reached the far side of the wire-mesh strip and moved along its fringe towards the tin-roofed office hut. The moonlight glinted on the blue Marchetti and Lucas Harrald's twin-engined Dove, once again side by side at the apron's edge. He moved closer, then swore softly at the dull glow of a dying fire. It came from a tiny hollow in the middle distance between the two aircraft and the office hut.

The next few yards he covered with infinite care, crouching low. Then, suddenly, he saw what was ahead and relaxed. The glow came from a low-slung charcoal brazier. On the ground beside it, wrapped snug in a heavy blanket, an elderly Moyallan watchman lay peacefully asleep.

Cord eased back, chuckled softly at his luck, and padded across to the hut's moonlit doorway. The lock was a simple spring-lever type — a few seconds gentle probing with one of the folding knife's smallest blades, a twist, and the tongue clicked back. He stepped inside, closed the door quietly behind him, and let the pen-torch's tiny beam flit rapidly round the room.

A low whisper of sound broke the silence and he jerked the torch in its direction. The beer refrigerator gleamed in the light and its motor ran for a few more seconds before it cut out. Another, fainter whisper followed in a moment or two and also stopped.

"You'd make one hell of a burglar," he muttered, then crossed to the first of the filing cabinets. It wasn't locked. The drawers held a jumble of office equipment, crumpled, unused forms and a pair of torn, oil-stained overalls. The other cabinet contained an equal confusion of tools, and empty beer bottles. He closed the last drawer, swung the pencil beam towards the desk while the 'fridge motor purred once more and was followed by that same, echoing whisper.

He waited till the quiet, steady note of his breathing was the only thing that broke the silence, then carried on.

The desk was locked, but another probing with one of the knife's pick-blades took care of that problem. He checked the drawers rapidly, and gave a soft sigh of satisfaction as he found the thick, hard-covered ledger labelled

'Movement Log — El Wabir'. The whispers of noise sounded again behind him, but he ignored them, opened the ledger, and began scanning its pages.

Johann Balder's records were stained, untidy, but reasonably complete. Landings and take-offs were faithfully recorded with aircraft registration numbers, owners, dates and times, plus services supplied. Traffic was light at El Wabir Sometimes a couple of days passed without any note of an arrival or departure, usually a single page was enough to record a week's activity.

Only three registration numbers were recorded with any real frequency. The Free Skies Airline's D.C.3 had made its thrice weekly calls, Lucas Darrald's Executive Dove appeared on its regular comings and goings, and there were more occasional visits by the U.N. operated Marchetti air-taxi. The rest could be counted on the fingers of one hand — Mid-Con Petroleum charters, a few Moyallan government flights and a rare visit from the southern district's air ambulance.

Gnawing gently on his lip, Cord concentrated on the most recent entries. The day the D.C.3 had crashed, Balder had drawn a heavy double line down each side of the page. The Free Skies transport had spent four hours on the airstrip between arrival and departure, had drawn 500 gallons of fuel, and was listed as having delivered mail and general cargo.

Underneath the take-off details Balder had written one short sentence . . . 'Crashed one minute after airborne, no survivors."

But there was something wrong. While the other pages had their entries smudged or smeared, sometimes in ink, sometimes in pencil, this page was different. All its entries were in the one ink, with none of the untidy overlapping so typical of the rest. It was as if the five days it recorded had been written up as one.

The whisper from the direction of

the refrigerator sounded again as he examined the logbook with a new care. It was a good quality job, its sheets made up in sections of sixteen pages, each section first linen stitched then threaded to a central spine. He had to check twice in the narrow beam of the pen-torch before he was sure. Only twelve pages remained in the plane-crash segment. Someone had made a particularly neat job of removing the original page for the day of the crash along with its mate from the blank pages ahead.

Grimly satisfied, he closed the book. It was halfway back to the drawer when the whisper came again — this time close behind him, a rustle of movement followed by a low, angry hiss. He froze, a cold realisation which came very close to fear flooding through his veins.

And further off, from the doorway, a voice broke through his tension. The words were low, quiet, yet steady in their warning.

"Stay very still, Mr Cord. Do not

turn your head or move in any way. Not till I have dealt with something very close to your right leg."

As if angered by the intrusion, the whisper and hiss sounded again, louder and nearer. Cord forced every muscle to stay rigid while a gradually widening shaft of moonlight swept across the little hut as the door opened wider.

"There is a small snake," said the voice again, carefully, precisely. "It is small but nasty. Please, Mr Cord, very still."

He heard one soft footstep, another, then another — and the hiss grew in anger. The man approaching drew a deep breath, there was a soft thud, the quick, heavy stamping of a shoe, and another deep breath — but this time it was released as a sigh of relief.

"Turn now, Mr Cord."

He obeyed. A small, squat African stood less than a yard away in the moonlit room, his right hand resting lightly on the butt of a heavy Webley automatic holstered at his waist. On the floor beneath them lay a dark blue uniform jacket with a single silver bar on each shoulder. The man's face stayed impassive as, keeping his eyes fixed on Cord, he stooped to lift the jacket.

Underneath, lying like a piece of old and twisted rope, the snake was less than a yard long and no thicker than one of Cord's cheroots. Except for the head — it had been crushed flat, one poison fang still projecting in mute menace. As Cord watched, the tail gave a faint, final twitch.

"A young ring-hals," said his rescuer softly. "I am sorry, Mr Cord. I was at the door for a little while. But though you left it unlocked I had to wait, to be sure of where this was before I could act."

"Better late than never," said Cord, his mouth still dry.

The broad face parted in a brief, white-toothed grin. "*Ahasante* . . . thank you. I am David Saat, and I would suggest we tidy up and leave. It would not do for a district inspector of police to be found in . . . well, such circumstances."

Wordlessly, Cord replaced the ledger, locked the desk again, then glanced up. "What about the snake?"

"I have collected it," said the policeman, a wisp of satisfied humour in his voice as he shrugged his way into his uniform jacket. "It is an old trick. A watchman can sleep peacefully when others know he has left his little friend on duty. There is not an African in El Wabir who would try to steal from this place at night. Now — well, he will wonder. But nothing will be missing, he would not want the Bwana Balder to know how he keeps watch. So he will simply go looking for a new little friend to replace the one which slipped away. Shall we go now, Mr Cord — "

Cord nodded and led the way. Once they were out, he used the knife-blade to relock the door while the African watched with professional interest. When it was done, Saat bent down, collected a matching blue beret from where he'd left it on the porch, and was ready.

"Our watchman will still be sound asleep," he murmured. "But this time I suggest I lead the way."

Three hundred yards from the airstrip's boundary, already deep into the patchy bush and tall, coarse *ban* grass, Saat stopped, whirled the dead ring-hals swiftly around his head, and let it fly off into the night. Then he set a fast, steady pace for another half mile before he stopped beside a massive clump of thorn and squatted down to rest.

"*Sasa* . . . this should be far enough."

Cord sank down beside him, took one of the cigarettes the Moyallan offered from a small tin box, and accepted a light from a match held between the man's cupped hands. He drew on it with a thankful sigh.

"Thanks again for what happened back there."

Saat gave an embarrassed shrug,

removed his beret, and rubbed his scalp for a moment. His heavy, thick-lipped features scowled a little. "It would have been awkward for a U.N. official, particularly a European, to be found dead in such circumstances." He puffed briefly on his own cigarette and let the smoke filter down his broad nostrils. "I do not like such things in my district."

"That's understandable," agreed Cord dryly. "Don't tell me you just happened to be passing."

"It is simple enough. I had an interest in you, I waited outside John Spence's house, you left and I followed." The policeman wriggled his holster into a more comfortable position. "Mr Cord, maybe I should believe you are here to talk about seed quotas and cattle. But I am the man who reported to my superiors on the aircraft which fell into Lake Calu. I am also the man who received a priority order to confirm the details I had sent. When I have done this there is silence — silence until you arrive." He gave a heavy frown. "Should I pretend I was surprised when you broke into that hut?"

"My people have a special interest in the crash," said Cord warily. He wondered briefly about this Moyallan — his background, whether he was married, where he'd learned that careful, slightly ponderous English, how he coped with a district as vast and lonely as Lake Calu.

Saat grunted. "Because the *Tillik Sau* Darrald's son was aboard?"

"No." Cord made his decision. "There was a man on that plane who had two fingers missing from one hand. You remember him?"

"A worker — yes, I know the one." Saat was puzzled. "When the body was found the travel paper in his pocket gave his name as Falea. But a worker, a labourer going back to his village?"

"He had another name and another task. His death may have been convenient to someone." Cord stubbed the half-smoked cigarette into the dusty soil. "I knew him well."

"Mr Cord, there were twenty-six men — "

He cut the Moyallan short. "And many have died before now so that an insurance policy could be cashed. This was more important."

Saat muttered briefly under his breath then leaned forward. "Mr Cord, all I know of this crash makes the picture of an accident. That there were so many aboard, *ni, mauti* . . . it was fate. Both the oil company and Lucas Darrald bring men here to work on contract, and fly them in and out because it costs less. It happened that two batches of contract-expired men were on the same flight."

"What about the one you called Falea?"

"He was with the Mid-Con Petroleum party."

"You're sure?"

"As sure as with any of the bodies. Identification was not easy. In this part of Moyalla crocodiles are not the only things which swim in water and have — well, unfortunate habits. With him, of course, the fingers helped."

Cord nodded a cold understanding. "Young Darrald's body is still missing isn't it?"

"His and some others," confirmed Saat "The plane itself may hold them. But the lake is deep. The airline people say raising it would be impossible without special equipment and great expense."

"Lucas Darrald hasn't suggested it?"

"Not yet. He is a practical man, even when he mourns." The Moyallan sucked his teeth. "Now it is my turn, Mr Cord. What interested you so much in the airstrip office?"

"Some background information, nothing more," lied Cord easily. "I didn't know I was going to make such rapid contact with the local police."

"And had no real wish to?" Saat didn't wait for an answer. A flicker of anger crossed his face. "This is my district. I could still decide you should be arrested for this night's work."

"But you won't," said Cord calmly.

"*Hapana* . . . no. Perhaps because I am too interested." The Moyallan rubbed a hand across his face. "If this Falea worked for the oil company, could it mean some of their people are involved?"

"I don't know. I wish I did." Cord eyed him keenly. "How do you rate Hal Berry, Inspector?"

"The land-train driver?" Saat frowned. "You make it plain you can say little, Mr Cord. In a different way, that also is my position. Except — "

"Well?"

Saat shook his head and suddenly rose to his feet. "It is late and I have a wife who worries. To reach John Spence's compound from here you travel — so." His hand gestured eastward. He waited until Cord got up. "Goodnight, Mr Cord. Or perhaps better, good morning."

Without another glance he strode off, his dark figure quickly blending and disappearing into the shadowed bush.

★ ★ ★

It was later than 3 a.m. when Talos Cord slipped back into his room in John Spence's house and almost nine before he wakened, the morning sun streaming through the window with a harsh, bright intensity and the temperature already climbing. Once he'd washed and dressed, he went through to the living room.

"Bwana Spence has gone," said the waiting Silda cheerfully. "He says for you to take the jeep when you want and that the keys are in it. You would like breakfast?"

"Just coffee," said Cord, yawning and settling in one of the chairs by the table.

"No more?" The houseboy showed his surprise, but obeyed.

When it came, black and steaming, Cord drank the first cup straight away, nursed his way through a second, and gave himself time to think.

A very good reason had brought Robert Tollogo from Tanzania to work on the Mid-Con payroll. Yet not once had he been able to get a message out to Andrew Beck. Because he'd been close — perhaps too close — to the munitions network?

And the Mid-Con people at El Wabir? He took clinical care to balance out Jean Berry's personal attractions. There was her brother, with his land-train on its regular supply journeys. First from Spence and then from Saat he'd caught more than a hint of reticence when it came to the name of Hal Berry. Add Johann Balder's doctored logbook at the Mid-Con airstrip and there was plenty of cause for suspicion.

Yet if the two Mid-Con men were involved they were still only a minor part of the pattern. Something very much bigger lay behind them.

Lucas Darrald was big — but his

only son had been aboard that D.C.3.

It didn't make sense.

He left the coffee and crossed to Spence's transmitter. It took a minute or two to code out the message, a little longer to snap the switches, check the frequencies and let the radio warm up. There was a further frustrating wait before he could raise the U.N. duty operator at Nygall.

But when Talos Cord finally left the compound, started the waiting jeep and set off on the dusty track to El Wabir he could be sure of one thing. From U.N. headquarters at the Moyallan capital, to Rome and on to New York his message was now on its way to Field Reconnaissance. If there was anything Andrew Beck could turn up on Hal Berry a reply would be back before the day was done.

In between times, his sister seemed well worth another call.

★ ★ ★

Jean Berry was in the front office of the Mid-Con building, using a slow but dogged two-finger technique on a studio model typewriter. She looked up as the door opened and Cord entered, greeted him with a smile, and pushed the machine aside with a sigh of relief.

"One day I'm going to throw that thing through the nearest window," she promised, relaxing back. "Finding your way around all right, Talos?"

"I haven't had to shout for help, if that's what you mean." He lifted the counter flap, came over to the desk, and glanced at the sheet of paper in the machine. "Important?"

"Weekly payroll sheets for the drilling sites — Hal has to take them out next trip."

Casually, as if only mildly interested, he read down the list of names. "All native labour?"

She nodded. "They're the contract squads. Company staff have their pay banked, can cash credits for what they

67

need, and the balance lies drawing interest."

"Lucky staff." He tapped the list thoughtfully. "This sort of thing could help my survey — rates of pay, numbers of native labour, local percentage as opposed to men brought in from outside — "

"It won't help as much as you imagine," she warned. "Unless a contract labourer wants an allotment paid direct to his home village — and few of them do — all we'll have is his name and whatever country he claims to belong to."

"I'd still like to run through them."

"All right." Jean Berry crossed to one of the counter cabinets, opened it, and brought out a thick file. "These are copies of the last six months' paysheets. Help yourself."

She stood at his shoulder, near enough for her light, fresh perfume to tantalise his nostrils. Cord spread the file on the counter top and began skimming through the forms.

"What do these men actually do?" he asked.

"Well . . . " She pouted a little, considering. "There's about sixty on the payroll. As contract labour, we take them on for three months or so then they go back. Most of them only want to work for a season, then they get the call of home. They're labourers, camp boys, general help around the drilling sites — the lists are drawn up that way, by site numbers. Five sites, five sheets."

Cord nodded, only half-listening. He'd found what he wanted. A flicking back over a few sheets confirmed the rest. A Tanzanian named Wat Falea had joined the Mid-Con contract labour force a few days after Robert Tollogo had sent in his last report. The man had been assigned to drilling site three as a cook-boy at ten Moyallan dollars a week.

"Got the sort of thing you wanted?"

He looked up and nodded. "Fine. It all helps."

"Good." Jean Berry swung herself up on the edge of the counter, shoes swinging lightly an inch or two from the floor. "Funny thing — you remember we were talking about Lucas Darrald yesterday and I mentioned he had a daughter?"

"Named Paula," he agreed.

"Well, she's back. The *Tillik Sau* brought her in by plane from Nygall yesterday evening, which explains why Richarn Nyeme was at the airstrip when you arrived." She gave a broad grin of pleasure. "Well, I could use some female-type company around here."

"You've got Zeneb," said Cord, matching her mood.

"Who makes a wonderful old Mother Friday but that's it. She was reared at a mission school — the kind where they had to pray for their supper and were told if you liked a thing it was pretty nearly bound to be sinful." Her nose wrinkled. "About the only person I can talk and relax with in El Wabir is Mary Saat."

"The inspector's wife?"

She blinked. "That's right. How did you guess?"

"We — Spence mentioned his name last night."

"A gossip session at the compound?" Jean Berry's eyes twinkled. "I'd have thought you'd be talking shop." She stopped as the growing rumble of a powerful, low-geared engine came from along the street, then beckoned Cord over to the window. "Eleven o'clock truck time — one of our big events of the day."

There were two of them, heavy, high-sided giants, travelling slowly, forced low on their massive springs by the weight of their tarpaulin-covered loads. Painted dull green, sides streaked with a grey-white sludge, they kept going while villagers, children and assorted livestock moved reluctantly from the path of their giant wheels. From the cab of the leading truck, a grinning, bare-chested Moyallan driver and his mate kept up a cheerful exchange of insults with the indignant locals. The crew of the following truck picked up the shouted threads and added their own contributions.

Cord watched until both vehicles had rumbled past, leaving a blue fog of exhaust fumes hanging in the air.

"Boss Darrald's?" he queried.

She nodded, with a slight but unmistakable frown. "Two trucks a day every day at this time. He's a stickler for routine. They're on their way to the coast — he's got a small fleet of them operating on a shuttle service."

"How long for the round trip, Jean?"

"He ships out of one of the smaller ports down the coast — it's about a three day trip there and back."

Cord raised an eyebrow. "Something annoys you about it?"

"No, not something." He hesitated and flushed a little. "Someone — Darrald's manager at the chemical site. He — well, we just don't get on."

He saw she wouldn't say more, and

changed the subject. "Mind if I look in tonight on the chance your brother is back?"

"Of course not. But leave it till fairly late if you want to be sure of getting him." One hand straying to the throat of her shirt-blouse, she asked, "What's on your schedule till then?"

He grimaced. "I'm not sure. I'm still interested in having a meeting with Lucas Darrald."

"You can always try." She considered the idea. "With Paula back things may be easier."

"How do I get to his place?"

"Simple enough. Take the spur road from the west end of the village and keep on going. It's about half an hour's drive and impossible to miss."

He thanked her and left. Outside, he stopped long enough to light a cheroot then crossed the dusty street and swung himself aboard the jeep. The seat was blistering hot from its wait in the open, and sweat formed on the palms of his hands as he started the engine.

A call on Lucas Darrald was the natural choice. Still, there was something else he should do. Maybe David Saat had been right and the old watchman at the airstrip would say nothing about the loss of his snake. But it was worth checking.

Cord chewed gently on the cheroot as he set the jeep moving. He was thinking of the easy, unworried way in which Jean Berry had handed him those pay-roll sheets. They'd given one more lead to Robert Tollogo's movements.

He frowned, horn-blasted a stray chicken, and corrected himself. They'd told him something else. The girl was unaware that anything required hiding.

But at the end of the day, if her brother was involved? Cord knew better than to even attempt to guess her reaction. In his book, no two women had minds which worked the same way in that kind of crisis.

It was eleven fifteen by his watch when the jeep bounced across the *ban* grass track and reached the airstrip.

At first it seemed deserted, but as he pulled to a halt a solitary figure hurried towards him from the parked aircraft.

Paul Duvert's face was a study in outraged impatience. The U.N. pilot's voice came as a splutter as he reached the vehicle.

"If you are looking for that idiot Johann Balder, m'sieu, all I can say is good luck!"

Cord left the jeep, tossed away the stub of his cheroot, and looked around. "What's the problem?"

"Problem?" The man spluttered again. "For me there is none. I can take off and wave goodbye to this little part of tomorrow land. I should have done so half an hour ago." He spread his hands in despair. "But I was stupid enough to agree to carry some parcel for Balder, a parcel he wants delivered in Nygall. Yet what do I find? No Balder, not even that long, miserable devil Wani is anywhere around." He swore briefly. "So now I have waited enough. If you see him, m'sieu, please tell him."

"All right." Cord felt a vague uneasiness at the situation, but kept his voice cheerfully amused. "When's your next call here?"

"A couple of days, perhaps." The Frenchman's scowl melted to a sly grin. "Tell me, m'sieu, what did you think of the little surprise that waited at the Mid-Con office?"

"Nice, very nice."

Duvert winked. "My feelings are the same." He grinned again, turned, and strode off towards his aircraft. Once aboard, he waved briefly from the cockpit then the engine fired. A minute later the Marchetti began rolling, passed the hut in a minor gale of slipstream dust, roared along the mesh strip, and took off in a fast, high-angled climb. As the drone faded, Cord frowned at the little hut, rubbed his chin, then turned back towards the jeep.

A horn blared before he could climb aboard. A dark blue long-wheelbase Land Rover was bustling towards him from the direction of the village, two uniformed askaris clinging to the hood arches, a third driving, and a familiar squat-shouldered figure peering through the windscreen from the front passenger seat. District Inspector Saat was in a hurry.

Cord stayed where he was. The Land-Rover skidded to a halt in front of the jeep, the passenger door flew open, and Saat jumped den. He barked an order to the rest of the Land-Rover's crew, then came across and stopped, the short fly-whisk in his left hand swinging ominously.

"Good-morning." Cord waited cautiously while the African inspected him with a cold stare.

"Who was in that 'plane, Mr Cord?" said Saat eventually.

"Just the pilot — "

"Duvert? No one else?"

"I didn't look under the back seat, if that's what you mean." Cord slipped one hand under his jacket, reaching towards his shirt pocket. A familiar click sounded behind the jeep, and he turned his head. An Askari was standing less than a yard behind him, the muzzle of an F.N. automatic rifle pointed straight at his head, the safety catch firmly at the 'off' position.

He looked back at Saat. "Better tell your constable that if he fires from there the bullet will go through me, then you, and end up making a nice round hole in your Land-Rover."

Saat's mouth twitched briefly, then he gave a flick of the fly-whisk. "*Hapana . . . endelea.*" The catch clicked again and the askari reluctantly stalked away to where his companions were gathered near the office hut.

Cord felt in his shirt pocket, brought out two of the cheroots and offered one towards Saat. The Moyallan shook his head.

"We are looking for a man, Mr Cord."

"Me?"

"The man Wani." Saat took a deep, angry breath. "Half an hour ago a woman came in from the bush. She goes daily to clean house for the airstrip man Balder, but this morning, when she arrived, there were vultures gathered outside his home. When she got closer, she saw what had attracted them — and since then I have seen."

"Balder?" Cord's face changed to a tight, grim mask.

"Balder," nodded the Moyallan. "It was either a panga knife or an axe, Mr Cord. But it did its job well."

"I see." Cord slid the cheroots back into his pocket. "And you think Wani is your killer?"

"That is at least how it looks." Saat folded his arms, his heavy lips pouting their anger. "His woman says he did not come to their hut last night. All I know is that he was seen drinking in the beerhalls — and boasting how little he thought of white men."

"Which is no crime, unless he translated words into deeds," said Cord slowly. "Well, Duvert's on his way to Nygall. But he was looking for either Balder or Wani before he left, and

79

kicking up a row because they weren't around."

Saat grunted, then turned aside as one of the askariz returned. The man, a lanky, hollow-cheeked veteran, spoke briefly, shook his head vigorously to Saat's questions, and then set off, shouting to the others to return.

"No trace of him," said Saat bitterly. "All they can find are the footprints of two men with shoes who went from the hut to the bush. I have told him that — that they can be ignored." His eyes hardened. "But perhaps I should not be so sure, Mr Cord. You have not been here twenty-four hours and already trouble has begun."

"You think I'd something to do with it."

"No. Not directly — but it has still happened." The askaris were back in the Land-Rover and waiting. "I think you should see for yourself, Mr Cord."

"I think I'd better," agreed Cord softly.

The Moyallan looked at him for a moment, nodded, then swung himself into the jeep's passenger seat with a violence which made the springs creak. Cord climbed in, took the wheel, started the engine, then glanced at his passenger.

"We will lead." Saat waved his whisk in a signal to the Land-Rover then settled back with a stoney expression on his face. "Head north, Mr Cord."

They drove off, the police vehicle swinging behind into their dust-trail.

★ ★ ★

Johann Balder had lived alone in a three-roomed mud-brick house set about a mile from the landing strip. The reason for the house's site was self-evident from the litter of rubble and disused concrete foundations which lay around — this was where Mid-Con Petroleum had made its first, abortive site location when they tried to find natural gas around Lake Calu, with the house erected as the site manager's quarters.

The blue-jerseyed askari who'd been sitting on the verandah steps picked up his rifle and scrambled to his feet as the jeep and Land-Rover came up the track towards the house. He squared his shoulder and moved into position beside the blanket-covered shape a few yards away.

Cord switched off the Jeep's engine and followed his passenger to the spot. Saat stopped beside the blanket and used his whisk as a pointer. Words weren't necessary — bloodstains on the earth around told their own story. Balder had been attacked near the door of the house and had covered only a short distance before he'd gone down.

For the moment, the vultures had gone. But a single great Marabou stork circled lazily overhead, and a trio of carrion crows perched on the house roof with tireless patience.

Lips pursed, Cord lifted one corner of the blanket. Balder lay on his front, his face twisted to one side, his skull opened by one blow, a second gaping wound high on his right shoulder. There had been strength behind the blows — and the blade of a heavy, saw-backed panga would do the rest. He looked at the rest of the body. Balder wore a pyjama top, but the lower half of his body was in his usual khaki drill trousers. The shoes on his feet had their laces knotted.

"Well?" David Saat stood with his legs a little apart, his eyes fixed on the crows.

Cord replaced the blanket and shrugged. "I'd say he had a visitor, someone he knew, and was in no rush to get dressed, otherwise he wouldn't have stopped to tie these shoelaces. After that — who knows?"

Saat nodded. "You speak as I expected, like a man who has seen such things before," he said dryly. "Out here, without experts, it would be difficult to be too precise about when it happened. But from the little I can do I would say the time of death was about three this morning — roughly when you would be arriving at John Spence's compound."

"You've checked I did?"

"Of course. The houseboy confirms it — he was instructed to watch." The Moyallan dismissed the matter. "Now, inside."

He led the way. The main room was simply furnished, with an old leather armchair drawn up beside a table and an ancient battery radio. A half-empty bottle, a used glass and the uncleared traces of a meal were scattered around the table, already buzzing with flies. At the rear, one doorway led to a tiny kitchen with a cooking stove, a small, chipped sink and a rusty water pump. The other, its curtain drawn back, led into Balder's bedroom.

Bed and bedding were in disorder, the mattress ripped open along its length, the pillow similarly treated. A wooden trunk had been dragged out into the centre of the floor and its lid forced open.

Cord glanced questioningly at the policeman.

"As we found it," said Saat briefly.

Inside the trunk, a thin leather briefcase had been cut open and its contents spilled around. Saat reached down, picked up a thin green-covered booklet and handed it to Cord. "This puzzles me — can you say what it is?"

Cord flicked it open. On the inner cover, under a heavy, eagle crest, was a passport-type photograph of a serious-faced young man in air force uniform, pilot's wings on the breast pocket of his tunic. He turned to the other pages then closed it gently.

"Once upon a time, after World War Two, they issued these to Poles who'd fought with the allies and felt it wouldn't be healthy to go home. According to this he had no known relatives."

The rest of the papers were old letters and souvenirs. Underneath, poking up from a torn crumple of tissue paper, he glimpsed a familiar colour of cloth. He parted the tissue with a sigh, guessing what he'd find. The air force uniform smelled strongly of mothballs but was still as clean and uncreased as the day it had first been laid away.

"No man is without his past," murmured Saat almost to himself. "Certainly, I am not — nor you, Mr Cord. Am I right?"

Cord said nothing and slowly shut the lid of the trunk. Gay heroes could find life difficult when glory was in short supply and they had to grow old — there were plenty of men who'd been like Johann Balder and had followed the same grey journey.

"From the practical viewpoint it is good there are no relatives," declared Saat, speaking quickly as if to cover a sudden embarrassment. "For the rest, I will take care of the details. And so we have a quarrel, an argument perhaps, a drunken man — maybe two drunken men." He rested his chin on the tip of the fly-whisk. "Would you agree?"

"Maybe." Cord turned his back on

the trunk. There was little sense in searching the room. Whoever had been there before them had made a thorough job of it already.

The Moyallan seemed to read his mind. "You are not so sure, Mr Cord. Perhaps you are wondering if someone else saw us last night — someone else who had a reason to come here and silence this man." The fly-whisk slapped against his side. "You expect me to ignore the smell of coincidence in my nostrils?"

Reluctantly, Cord shook his head. "I can't help you, Inspector — not yet. If I tried to I might be wrong, and involve you in a mistake so big you'd lose that uniform altogether. It might be something your government had its own view about."

Saat was unperturbed. "I am not a politician. Such considerations do not concern me."

"If you believe that you're a fool." Cord saw the man's eyes harden and knew it had hurt. "Especially now, when your government is doing a tight-rope act with the army as its only balancing pole. They're sensitive to anything that smells of trouble."

"A man's murder means nothing to you?" demanded the Moyallan acidly. "Not this man, not the one on the plane, or the others?"

"I didn't come to Lake Calu to find out how the man on the plane was killed, but why," said Cord wearily.

"He was — " Saat scowled as he fumbled for the word — "expendible?"

"He was a friend, and his name was Robert Tollogo," corrected Cord softly. "But he was doing a job."

"*Ndio* . . . and now you are to finish it?" Saat looked at him for a long minute, the expression on his face slowly changing. Then, suddenly he nodded. "All right, Mr Cord. Tell me when you can. Somehow I think I might not like to find that you too had become — expendible." He brightened. "For the moment, we will look for this man Wani. He may be the simple explanation, or part of a more difficult one. If he has run off into the bush, or joined some *shifta* band, it will not be easy. But we will try."

"Did Balder have a car?"

"Yes, an old Volkswagen — it is round at the back." He led the way once more. The car's doors were closed but unlocked, the ignition key was in place. When Cord tried it, the fuel gauge registered an almost full tank.

"I am a little surprised the car was not taken, but — " Saat shrugged his weary acceptance. "Who can tell about such things?" As they started to retrace their steps, he asked, "If there is reason to contact you, Mr Cord, where will you be?"

"Travelling around," said Cord bleakly. "But I'll be at the Mid-Con office tonight. I'm due to meet Hal Berry."

"Ah — " Saat nodded wisely. "He returns with the land-train, of course. I have already spoken to his sister of this and told her there is nothing that cannot wait until then."

Cord left him standing by the verandah and went back to the jeep. He started the engine, revved it savagely, and slammed it into gear.

There was just one thing David Saat didn't seem to have seen. The leather of Johann Balder's scuffed, down-at-heel shoes had been streaked with a grey-white staining — a staining Cord had only seen once before in the Lake Calu area, on the trucks which had passed hauling their loads of chemical to the outside world.

Robert Tollogo might have died because he was on the oil company's payroll. But Johann Balder had been somewhere near that chemical plant last night. And not, apparently, in the Volkswagen. It's tyres were clean.

Just why might be important.

3

THE spur road to Lucas Darrald's domain spent its first few miles never far from the shore of Lake Calu. That meant scattered, thatched-roofed farmsteads, close-ups of sandbar-shallows, and an occasional glimpse of livestock. But then it swung inland, the farmsteads quickly thinned, the *ban* grass yellowed, and the first thorn-trees clawed grotesquely from the arid soil.

Eyes narrowed against the harsh, shimmering blue of the sky, mouth and nostrils lined with the dust thrown up by the jeep's passage, Talos Cord drove steadily, avoiding the worst of the potholes. He could feel the scorching heat strike him in waves, could sense the utter emptiness of the land around him, and cursed softly at the luck which had brought him to this corner of Moyalla.

The jeep growled on, the miles clicked by, and the first low hills began to grow in the distance. Their slopes became a light, heat-tormented veil of green, then gradually firmed into the fringe of the cedar-wood forest which ran from there far back into the high country.

At last, with the hills looming close, a long, planted windbreak of pink-flowered mimosa told him he'd reached his destination — and Cord's eyes widened as the jeep rounded a turn and he saw the great, sprawling house which lay ahead.

House was maybe not the word. A long, low structure, built of brick, fringed by outbuildings, it was more like some old-style fort. From a wide, high-arched central gateway the rest swept back in a hollow square. A flat roof, one high central tower and a broad gravelled driveway bounded by a wooden fence all helped the illusion. All that seemed missing was a flagpole and sentry.

He left the spur road, motored the jeep slowly up the drive, and parked to the left of the gateway. As he got out, a lithe figure strode towards him from the inner courtyard.

"*Salaam* and welcome, Mr Cord." Richarn Nyeme's fine-boned features held more of a frown than a welcome. His handshake was brief and light. "I saw the jeep turn for here, and wondered who it might be." He forced the makings of a smile. "Mr Darrald didn't mention — "

"This isn't an official visit," explained Cord easily. "But I've started looking around the district. It seemed a reasonable idea to call in."

"Of course." Nyeme glanced briefly at his watch. "There's just a chance the *Tillik Sau* might see you, though he has been busy. His daughter — "

"I heard she'd arrived," nodded Cord. He let a brief grimace cross his face. "Maybe this isn't a good time to come calling, but I had an unpleasant start to my day. Driving here was a good excuse to get away from your local police inspector."

Nyeme raised a polite but interested eyebrow. "Because of what happened to Johann Balder?" he asked unexpectedly. "We've heard. A couple of our men brought the news back from the village. But — how does it concern you, Mr Cord? The story I was told said they were hunting for Balder's man Wani."

"They still are." Cord put indignation into his voice. "But Inspector Saat wanted a European along when he checked through Balder's home, and I happened to be handy."

"David Saat would make an excellent if somewhat old-fashioned diplomat," murmured Nyeme with a faint scowl. "He believes in — I think the phrase is 'Racial harmony'. Sometimes he carries it too far." He shook his head. "Balder was no great asset at the airstrip, but it is still a tragedy. *Ni mauti* . . . I will find out — if Mr Darrald is free."

Cord followed him through the brief shadow of the archway into the inner courtyard. It was paved in brick, with a few shrubs in a central ornamental plot. A houseboy was sweeping round its edge with a twig broom, humming softly as he worked.

"What's up there?" asked Cord, thumbing towards the tower.

Nyeme shrugged. "Very little. The first building here was a mission church, run by some well-meaning English. That was to have been their bell tower, but they ran out of money. Lucas Darrald rebuilt the rest, but the tower — well, it does no harm." A brief shadow crossed his face. "When I was young his son and I would go up there. It made a fine place for boys to play."

From the courtyard they went through a low door into a broad, cool hallway. The coffee-skinned Moyallan ushered Cord into a long, narrow room and gestured around. "My office — perhaps you know, my main role is as Mr Darrald's accountant. If you will wait, I will see what can be done."

Once he'd left, Cord inspected his surroundings. Nyeme's tastes formed an odd mixture. The desk was of chrome and steel, with chairs to match its modern lines. A vacuum jug of iced water and a small adding machine completed the businesslike air. But the wood-block floor had skin rugs scattered over its surface and the walls were decorated with broadbladed spears, a long, cane-framed fighting shield and a couple of viciously spiked iron clubs.

He moved to the window, which overlooked the courtyard. The native sweeper had disappeared, but as he watched another of the house doors swung open. The girl who came out into the sunlight brought a soft, unsummoned whistle to his lips. Tall and slim, with short, corn-stray coloured hair, she wore a white linen dress with a silver chain belt and low-heeled sandals. Paula Darrald walked quickly across the open space, giving him a glimpse of a firm-mouthed, slightly angry face. Then a door slammed on his side of the house and she had gone.

He was back studying the wall-mounted weapons when Nyeme at last returned.

"Well, you're in luck." The man seemed a little more relaxed than before. "Mr Darrald will be along in a few minutes."

"Good." Cord tapped the surface of the fighting shield. "You've a nice collection of these things."

"Primitive items, but effective in the right hands." Nyeme's voice held a brief glint of pride. "My people were a fighting race until a generation or two back."

"But not any more?"

"It is no longer necessary." Nyeme frowned uneasily as Cord moved on to examine one of the spears. "I would advise you against touching these, Mr Cord. My ancestors were enthusiastic in their use of poisoned spearheads. The juice from a certain beetle pupa — I looked it up once, the name is *diamphidia simplex* — was their favourite. Even when dry and old it can still be effective."

"Thanks for the warning." Cord grimaced, stepped back, and took the offered chair. Nyeme crossed over and fingered the keys of the adding machine in random fashion, as if part of his attention was elsewhere, waiting for something to happen. "Perhaps we can save some time, Mr Cord. I handle a good share of the estate's affairs — what would you like to know of our activities?"

"The general picture." Inwardly, Cord cursed the way he was trapped in this room. "Lucas Darrald seems to own quite a chunk of territory."

"He does." Nyeme turned from the adding machine, took a pack of cigarettes from his pocket, and lit one before answering. "On paper, the estate covers about two hundred square miles. But roughly half of that is hillside and empty bushland — kept very specifically as a wild life reserve.

Nearer home we have some farming acreage. But it counts for little — our main units are the timber and chemical operations."

Outside, distant but clearly audible, a vehicle engine pulsed to life. Cord saw the faint twitch which crossed the Moyallan accountant's face, but very deliberately relaxed back in his chair. "How many on the payroll?"

The vehicle — the engine note, though it kept low, was too heavy for a car — began drawing away. As it faded, the last load of worry seemed to be removed from Nyeme's shoulders.

"First, of course, there is the lumber operation, bringing out cedar from the foothills — we have about a hundred men working there. There are fewer, perhaps sixty in all, at the chemical pits."

"And that's where the money comes from," declared a gruff voice from the doorway. Cord turned, then rose to his feet as he saw the man who had entered the room, the fair-haired girl at his side.

"Mr Darrald?"

Lucas Darrald nodded. "My daughter, Paula," he said briefly.

The girl smiled a cool, polite greeting. Her father stayed where he was, feet wide apart. Small, thick-set, with greying hair and dark, piercing eyes, hands deep in the pockets of his lightweight fawn suit, he gave the immediate expression of a powerful little man, well aware that stature didn't have to be measured in physical inches.

Nyeme moved quickly towards him. "I was explaining — "

"I heard, Richarn." Darrald grunted briefly. "Well, Mr Cord, I didn't expect you to find your way here so quickly."

"Maybe I should have let you know first," he admitted.

"Why?" protested Paula, a needle of meaning in the glance she gave her father. "Unexpected visitors can be a pleasant surprise."

"Of course." The man's lined, square-jawed face tightened briefly. "And if you were thinking of my son's recent death, Cord, in this family we prefer to remember rather than mourn." He cleared his throat abruptly. "I gather you've had your own troubles this morning. Don't get the idea things like that happen often around here — Balder was the kind liable to end up that way."

"I only met him briefly, when I flew in yesterday," mused Cord. "He seemed harmless enough."

"My father will tell you an inefficient man is never harmless," said the girl cynically. She crossed to one of the chairs, sat down, and stretched her long, slim legs in lazy, cat-like fashion. "And Johann Balder certainly wasn't in top gear when we landed yesterday evening."

"I am afraid he was often that way," said Nyeme carefully. "It was, naturally, the last time we saw him."

Lucas Darrald followed his daughter's

101

example and took a chair by the window. He folded his arms, frowned with ill-concealed impatience, and demanded, "How much detail do you U.N. people need for this survey?"

"On this visit, only a broad outline."

"Which you should have been given before you came to Lake Calu," growled Darrald. "All right, the lumber operation is something I started fairly recently, and we're producing good quality timber. But haulage costs to the coast leave little over for profit. Our money-maker is something very different — soda ash, high grade sodium carbonate."

Cord nodded. That had been part of the briefing, along with the few details known of Lucas Darrald's background. Born in East Africa of Dutch descent, early success in a gold strike, now with a thriving trade producing a rich grade of the industrial chemical . . . a corner of his mind wondered again about the vehicle he'd heard departing.

"Glass, soap, paper — plenty of

industries need it." Darrald was lecturing now, enjoying a new, captive audience. "Years ago, just about the time I got married, I found what had once been the bed of an old, dried-up lake. Go down the spur road another few miles and you'll find it — a flat, grey waste. That's the crust of the old lake bed, a skin almost ten feet deep with an almost ninety per cent alkaline content.

"Dig up the crust and you've got what we call trona. Put the trona through a simple separation plant, and you're left with soda ash. It's an unglamorous product, but it brings in the money."

"The only good thing about it," said Paula with a surprising vehemence. "I hate the stuff."

Her father raised an eyebrow at the outburst, then turned back to Cord. "There's one other section here. I call it the Sanctuary."

"The nature reserve," nodded Nyeme. "I mentioned it earlier."

"Good." Darrald chose his words with a watchful care. "The soil's poor, there's nothing but rock, bush, and wild life. I think your survey can ignore it."

"Probably," said Cord slowly. "What you're really saying is 'keep off', isn't it?"

The makings of a grin crinkled the *Tillik Sau*'s leathery face. "Let's say I don't normally encourage visitors up there." He exchanged a brief, almost imperceptible glance with the Moyallan. "Still, give me a day or so and well, if you're interested I'll take you to the Sanctuary myself. But I'd better warn you not to try it on your own. I've one or two game wardens up there, and they can be rough with strangers. I keep it strictly private property."

"Don't the *shifta* gangs ever try to move in?" queried Cord.

"Those second-rate thugs?" Lucas Darrald snorted. "They stay clear of my land. They know better." He rose to his feet. "But don't misunderstand me. The Sanctuary apart, feel free to go anywhere."

"I myself would show you around," declared Nyeme earnestly. "But like Mr Darrald I have a full schedule for today. Perhaps tomorrow — "

"No need to wait." Paula Darrald smiled in a strangely bitter way as she gained their attention. "There's nothing on my schedule." She looked down at her dress and grimaced. "This is no outfit for jeep travel, but give me time to change, Mr Cord, and I'll take you on the grand tour." The girl threw a swift, defiant glance towards her father. "Unless there are objections."

Darrald gave a slow, bull-like shake of his head. "None from me — but I haven't heard what Cord feels about it. He's probably got plans of his own."

"Nothing that can't wait," said Cord cheerfully.

"Fine." The girl crossed to her father's side then promised from the doorway. "I'll be ten minutes, no more."

Once the Darralds had gone, Richarn Nyeme sighed and gave a quirk of a grin. "A young lady of determined character," he said dryly.

"Like her father?"

The Moyallan accountant nodded. "In many ways. He is a man who does not like his decisions challenged. When two such people meet — " he shrugged. "Now, while you wait, is there more I can tell you?"

"I'd settle for a look around the layout of this place," said Cord, watching for the man's reaction.

Nyeme gave it a moment's bland consideration and nodded. "Why not, Mr Cord? But — ah — I am afraid you will find little of interest."

With such unabashed willingness, the tour of the house and its outbuildings was inevitable in its everyday appearance. Living quarters for staff, storesheds, a well equipped garage-workshop, were all situated behind the main structure. A neat row of cars and utilities were parked on a concrete bay, one of them, a big, high-sprung Mercedes station wagon, being washed down by a couple of Darrald's outside staff.

Tractors and farming equipment, stacked fertilisers and a small but modern dairy yard — the rest was routine. If the Darrald place had its secrets they were well hidden. At last, Nyeme led Cord back to the courtyard, stopped near the arched gateway, shook him by the hand, and returned into the house.

Slowly, with a vague sense of anti-climax, Cord walked across the hot clean-swept bricks and out through the arched gateway. Then he brightened. Paula Darrald was already waiting in the jeep's passenger seat. She wore a bush shirt and tight blue denims laced into ankle-length boots. Her straw-coloured hair was held back from her forehead by a band of darker blue silk.

"Ready?" she asked.

"Ready," agreed Cord, swinging into the driver's seat and reaching for the ignition.

Whether or not anything was due to happen, he was going to have interesting company.

★ ★ ★

Back on the spur road, heading west along the rest of its length, the girl sat silent by his side and watched the passing scene through half-closed eyes.

"It never changes much," she said at last.

Cord turned his head briefly. "How long since you were home last?"

"About six months." One hand gripped the jeep's side as they took a bump and the springs heaved. "Do we have to be in such a hurry?"

"Sorry." He eased back a fraction on the accelerator. "You came back because of your brother, I suppose?"

She nodded. "As soon as I heard. But it took my father a couple of days to decide Frank was dead, and even then he made it a letter. I think he hoped — well, that it would all be over by the time I arrived. It makes it worse to be left wondering when you're going to hear a body has been washed up." Her voice remained steady and practical, but she gnawed a little on her lower lip before she went on. "Still, there's not much we can do about it."

Cord concentrated on the road for a moment. "Jean Berry told me you'd been away for a spell, but that's about all I know."

"Jean?" Paula Darrald brightened. "I haven't seen her since I got back. Like her?"

"Uh-huh. But I asked about you."

"That's easy enough." A strand of the corn-straw hair had escaped from her headband. She brushed it back. "It's a fairly common pattern. Shipped off to boarding school when I was a kid, then to university — back here for holidays, but little else. It makes it difficult to decide whether you've got roots anywhere. So every now and again I'm home for a spell then decide it's time to leave."

"Because of your father?"

She jerked indignantly. "What do you mean?"

"Just that from what I saw you rub each other like sandpaper," shrugged Cord.

"That?" She gave a lukewarm smile. "We — let's say we have our moments. But when I leave it's because this place has got on my nerves again and I want back among the pavements and people. Until — until this happened I had a flat in London and a job in a research plant."

They hadn't much further to go. As the jeep climbed a long, slow rise in the ground the vegetation around suddenly thinned and withered. At the top of the rise Cord saw what lay ahead and coasted to a halt.

From where the ground fell away in a wide, flat, saucer-like hollow — a hollow covered in a barren grey crust, like some obscene thin porridge which, once mixed, had been tipped over to spread in a shapeless monotony. The spur road ran across the saucer for about half a mile, ending beside a low cluster of buildings. Behind them lay the digging pits, long shallow gashes crisscrossing the crust, some partly filled with spoil, a few throwing back the sun's rays from the brackish water which had drained into them from the last, otherwise forgotten rains.

"Not very pretty, is it?" Paula Darrald leaned forward, switched off the jeep's engine, and the light wind brought a low rumble of machinery to their ears. She pointed to the largest of the buildings, veiled in a low pall of smoke-like dust. "That's the separation plant, first stage anyway. The trona from the pits goes through a screen and what you could call a riddle, then is fed into a crusher. What's left is the raw soda ash. The real chemical separation is something we leave to the buyers."

He nodded, watching a loaded, low-slung dump truck head from the pits towards the separator. Further out, at one of the long gashes in the dried-out lakebed, another truck waited while a bulldozer worked in team with a small mechanical shovel. "There's an old saying that where there's muck there's money."

"It's true," she agreed with a grimace. "The lake trona runs up to ninety per cent pure."

Not one tree, one bush, one patch of scrub — Cord turned away to face her. "I've seen pleasanter places," he admitted.

"I had my fill of it when I was younger," she said, her face tightening. "Some flamingoes had nested near one of the pits, where there was water. Then we found the young ones — dead. They couldn't fly, they'd spent too much time in the shallows. The soda crystals had dried round their legs like shackles and that was that." She forced her mind away from the memory. "Well, let's go down. We've a manager, Sydney Holt, and you'd better meet him."

Cord chuckled and started the jeep.

"I've heard about him from somewhere."

"From Jean?" Paula Darrald let a wisp of amusement cross her face. "I can imagine what she said. Still, he does a reasonable job of running the plant and he's got enough sense to behave himself with the boss's daughter."

"Always?"

"Let's say he learned the lesson." From the tone of her voice it was clear no doubts remained.

They drove down into the saucer, the noise of the crushing plant growing louder as they neared it, the billowing cloud of fine alkali grit soon stinging at their throats and eyes. Cord followed her directions and eventually brought the jeep to a halt outside a flat-roofed single storey hut built of cinder blocks.

"Give him a hoot," said the girl.

The horn bleeped, a white blob of a face appeared briefly at one of the grime-covered windows, and a moment later the hut door opened. The man who emerged beamed and crossed eagerly towards them.

"Our Sydney," Paula's voice was low and sardonic. "Uses the royal 'we' and almost believes it."

Sydney Holt looked in his early forties, a fussy, flabby man with a red face, mousey, carefully smoothed hair, and a gold filling in one of his front teeth. Despite the dust and the heat he wore a jacket and tie, and the muscles of his face continued to work overtime as he reached them.

"We're honoured, Miss Darrald — we heard last night you were back, but we didn't expect a visit so soon." The smile faded a few candlepower while she carried out the introductions, then brightened again. "Fine, Mr Cord. Anything we can do to help, and you've only to ask." He cocked his head to one side and the gold tooth flashed once more. "Perhaps you'd like to see our processing system?"

Cord thought briefly of the prospect of that grinding din at close quarters and shook his head. "Another day, maybe. Right now I'm just on a sight-seeing tour and meeting people."

"Of course." The plant manager nodded wisely and approvingly. "Preliminary introductions are always valuable. And you'll find that round Lake Calu we have quite a pleasant little social circle."

Paula Darrald made a strangled noise which became a cough. "Dust in my throat," she said hoarsely, keeping her face straight.

"Uh-huh." Cord was looking at the man's shoes. The leather was streaked with the same grey-white sludge as Johann Balder's shoes, a sludge that was something more than dust or grit.

Holt followed his gaze and pursed his lips in irritation. "We have what can be a messy job, I'm afraid. There's a water spray in the separator plant, to reduce the dust content on final loading — go anywhere near the loading bay and your feet get covered in this stuff."

"Sore on leather?"

"Burns through it in time," declared

Holt with a sigh. "I was saying to Mr Darrald the other day — "

Cord cut him short. "Is there a telephone out here?"

"Eh?" The man blinked. "No. Nothing like that. Why?"

"You said you'd heard last night that Miss Darrald had arrived. I wondered who told you."

"Oh." Holt's smile switched on in determined, almost self-protective reflex, but he eyed this sleepy-eyed, scar-cheeked stranger with a sudden wariness. "We — I just heard. One of the men — yes, that's right, one of the men told me. He'd been visiting some friend up at your father's house, Paula." He looked towards the girl for support, but Cord wasn't finished.

"You haven't had any news from there today — or from El Wabir?"

"No. Should I have?" Holt's smile faded again.

"Well — " Paula Darrald tried to answer, and was too late.

"Johann Balder was found dead this

116

morning." Cord brought the edge of one hand down on the flat palm of the other in brutal emphasis. "Someone used his head as a chopping block."

"I see . . . " the man's voice trailed away. Then he swallowed. "Who did it?"

Cord shrugged. "The police are looking for a native who helped him around the airstrip, a man called Wani. Seems he caused quite a turmoil in a beerhall last night saying just what he was going to do to Balder one of those days."

"The usual." Holt's red face regained its composure. "Plenty of them hate our guts, but they need us and they know it."

"Which can sometimes make them hate our guts all the more," murmured Paula, glancing impatiently in Cord's direction. "Time we were moving on. I promised my father I'd show Mr Cord the lumber camp on this trip, and that isn't just round the next corner."

"I'll take the hint." Obediently, Cord started the engine and gave Holt a vague salute. The plant manager made a cross between a nod and a bow in the girl's direction, mumbled his goodbyes, and stood back as the jeep meshed into gear and drew away.

* * *

They were more than a mile from the trona beds, heading along a rough, tyre-rutted track into the foothills, when Paula Darrald suddenly threw back her head and laughed in a way which sent a pulse throbbing at the base of her throat.

"What's so funny?" demanded Cord.

"Our Sydney and his 'pleasant little social circle'. Then you start talking about Balder's murder no wonder he was upset." She stopped laughing and frowned a little. "But what was so important about how he knew I'd arrived?"

"Just curiosity," he assured her

nonchalantly. "I like knowing how news travels."

"Around Lake Calu? Everybody knows everything practically before it happens. Gossiping is pretty high on the list of local amusements." Satisfied, she settled a little deeper into her seat.

The timber line began with a gradual thickening of the lesser scrub, now laced here and there by vivid green creepers. Then, only a thin scattering, the first of the tall, majestic Mlanji cedars made their appearance. The jeep climbed on, the gradual change continued, and soon the high, stately cedars ranked thickly on either side, at times so close one to another that their branches mingled in one dense overhead umbrella of foliage.

"Big — big and beautiful," mused Cord as the jeep rounded a bend and gave them a brief glimpse of still another stretch of forest ahead.

Paula nodded, and shifted her long, slim legs into a more comfortable position. "Frank used to come up here with Richarn Nyeme before we started timber cutting. They reckoned some of the really big ones were close to the hundred and fifty foot mark." She gestured over her shoulder. "Look, I don't know about you, but I'm hungry — and I brought some sandwiches. They're in the back. Suppose we have a quick look around the lumber camp, then have a break."

"You've got my vote," he agreed. It suddenly seemed a long time since he'd eaten.

Another mile brought them to the timber site, a long slope facing west a great scar of brown earth, naked stumps and stacked, cut logs. A power saw whined, a tractor was hauling two mighty trunks down towards the main clearing, and nearer at hand a noisy racket came from a de-barking machine as it stripped an earlier victim.

Cord threaded the jeep down the nearest of the rough paths which covered the site, noticing the cluster of crude bunkhouses halfway down.

They passed the first of the high stacks of waiting timber where a squad of the lumber gang were hard at work, the sweat glistening on their dark bodies.

"We send only cleaned cedar to the coast," explained the girl. "But the trimmings aren't wasted. We use them as boiler fuel at the soda plant." She broke off with a murmur of surprise and pointed ahead. "Look — we've got company."

Cord suppressed a groan as he saw the blue Land-Rover parked at an angle beside one of the loading platforms. An Askari driver lounged behind the wheel and District Inspector Saat was a little way on, standing beside a shaven-headed figure who topped him by several inches.

"That's Elagga, our foreman," said Paula as they drew nearer and the two men stared in their direction. "The hairstyle means he's a tribal elder — which comes in handy if we've a labour dispute."

The shaven head went with a thin,

long-nosed face, and the foreman emphasised his more professional authority by wearing a bright red shirt with khaki slacks which were tucked into a pair of ancient but well-polished thigh-length boots.

They parked close to the Land-Rover, got out and walked towards the men. The foreman grinned a gap-toothed welcome, but Saat contented himself with a polite, fractional bow.

"*Salaam*, Miss Darrald. It is good to see you home again," he said, glancing past her at Cord with eyes bright with a wary curiosity, the fly-whisk in his hand hanging slack by his side.

Paula smiled. "*Jambo*, David. All well at home?"

Saat thawed a little. "Including the new little one that you have not seen." His face parted in a brief smile. "We can expect you to visit, I hope?"

"I'll be along," she promised, then raised a questioning eyebrow. "I didn't expect to meet you out here."

The policeman gave a heavy-shouldered shrug. "Mr Cord will have told you of Johann Balder's death. The man Wani has friends here in the camp and might try to reach them. I thought it best to warn your foreman."

"I see." She glanced at the shaven-skulled elder. "Elagga, have you seen this man?"

"*Hapana*, Miss Paula!" The foreman gave a vigorous shake of his head and spoke in a quick, anxious voice. She listened, nodded, then translated for Cord's benefit. "He says his men wouldn't shelter such a villain. The local men, that is — but he wouldn't trust the outsiders."

"Personally, I wouldn't trust any of them," mused Saat. "But at least I have passed the warning."

"You think he's heading this way?" queried Cord.

The answer was a grim, cynical smile. "Maybe, maybe not — there is no report of him having been seen. But there is a routine to follow. He might try here, or the soda beds, perhaps even strike out for the drilling camps — anywhere."

"Maybe even the *Tillik Sau*'s nature reserve?" Cord glanced at the girl.

She shook her head. "He'd be foolish. Even if he managed to survive out there, the game rangers would spot him."

"He has already been foolish," reminded Saat, then shrugged. "But no, I think he would be more likely to try elsewhere, where he might get help. Anyway, I have much work to do. Goodbye, Miss Darrald — I will tell my wife we have met."

Cord watched him go, then cursed under his breath and hurried after the man, catching him up as he reached the vehicle. "Inspector, there are always the chemical trucks — the ones that left for the coast this morning."

"There are," agreed Saat dryly. "But they were stopped by my colleague in the next district. Wani was not aboard." He opened the Land-Rover's door, climbed aboard, and slammed it shut. His thick lips scowled from the open window. "Do you really think he has gone so far, Mr Cord?" The policeman shook his head. "Not if he was any part of what interests you, let us admit it. Which means that what interests you must very much interest me."

The fly-whisk waved briefly, the askari behind the wheel pressed the starter, and the Land-Rover drove off.

Cord sighed and walked back to where Paula was waiting.

"Just an idea I had," he said ruefully. "It was shot down quick enough."

She grimaced. "Then let's get back to the guided tour. Elagga has something he wants us to see."

The foreman led the way, taking a worn footpath which led up the hillside between the scattered stumps. Above and around them more of the timber gang were at work, loading lengths of the rich yellow-brown wood into stacks, trimming other branches with axe and saw. The air was filled with the scent of the fresh-cut cedar.

At last their guide stopped by one massive stump, grinned, and pointed. "This one, Missie Paula."

The girl gazed at it quizzically. "He counted the rings on the stump and reckons it exactly two hundred and twenty years old. That means it was a fair-sized tree long before the first European arrived in this part of the world."

"He said that?"

"No. I did." She laughed and gestured around her. "Well, what do you think of the place?"

"Impressive."

Satisfied, she sat down on the edge of the big, platform-like stump, took a slim silver cigarette case from her shirt pocket, clicked it open, and held it towards the foreman. He took a cigarette with a murmur of thanks, tucked it behind one ear, and moved a few paces away.

"Talos?"

He took one in turn, waited till she

was ready, then snapped his lighter to life. Her hands cupped briefly round the flame, then she leaned back with a sigh.

"What do you know about cedar, Talos?"

Cord remembered his Food and Agriculture role. "The basics are that it grows best in sandy loam, at a reasonable altitude — and that it's worth money."

"There's more," she mused. "Remember the Cedars of Lebanon, exalted above all the trees of the field'? In this country the Moyallans are like the Arabs — they've legends that the cedars can think and talk."

"But they don't object to cutting them down for cash," he reminded with a twinkle.

She ignored him. "Oil of cedar used to be something pretty precious for curing a whole variety of ills — including leprosy." She ran a hand over her hair, her face strangely thoughtful. "Frank and Richarn found some other things up here. They brought back a couple of scruffy looking hill plants — aromatics that happened to be frankincense and myrrh."

"You're going to miss your brother," he said quietly.

"Yes." Suddenly, her expression changed. She stubbed the cigarette viciously on the stump, got up, and became briskly business-like. "Let's get back, I'm hungry."

Together, they started back down the narrow track towards the jeep. A little more than halfway there, she stopped and frowned.

"I forgot — my father gave me a message for Elagga." She shook her head before he spoke. "Don't bother coming. I'll catch up on you." Next moment she had gone, hurrying back the way they'd come.

Cord strolled on, hands in his pockets, his face thoughtful. So far there was more than one reason why he should distrust Lucas Darrald's little empire. But this girl was a strange mixture, hard to place in any neat category.

He took an idle kick at a broken twig, then heard a rumble above him.

He spun round. Still spilling from their collapsing stack, the cords of cedar were as thick as a man's forearm and anything up to ten feet long. He had a vague impression of a figure scuttling back from the moving avalanche, heard high-pitched shouts coming from the men further along the slope, then the logs became a tumbling torrent — dozens of them, bumping, rolling, jolting, spilling high into the air.

The first instinct was to run. But the torrent was widely spread, moving too quickly. There was only one possible hope left, a hope which flashed at the same time as the first of the logs bounced less than twenty feet away. He sprang madly up the hill, as if to meet the torrent — than threw himself down behind the low shelter of the sawn-off tree stump, pulled his legs up close to his body, buried his head beneath his arms, and waited for the inevitable.

The leading log hit the stump end-on, cart-wheeled crazily, and kept going. The next smashed to a halt then the world was a clash and noise, a dust of bark fibres, a grating of splintering wood, a bewildering succession of grazing blows, the rip as a remnant of branch caught and tore the cloth of his shirt.

At last, after some of the longest seconds he'd ever known, there was silence.

"*Endelea . . . bwana . . . bwana . . .*" He lay dazed while the shouts reached his ears. The first of the lumber men pulled and dragged at the logs jammed around the stump then once they were cleared, helped him to his feet, muttering in wide-eyed surprise as they realised he was unhurt. Further down, the hill path had almost disappeared under a debris of wood.

Paula Darrald came running towards them then slowed for the last few yards, and stared at him in disbelief. "I thought . . . Talos, what happened?"

"That's what I'd like to know." Cord moved his limbs gently, decided nothing was broken, then winced as he turned. His back felt as if he'd been flogged.

Elagga arrived a moment later, panting for breath — and the camp foreman's face twitching with something close to fear as he met Cord's gaze.

"Ask him who the hell stacked that firewood," said Cord wearily.

Paula nodded and rapped the question. The shaven-headed elder clenched his teeth briefly and answered in an unhappy voice.

"Let me guess," said Cord sarcastically. "He doesn't know except that it wasn't him."

"That pretty well sums it up," said the girl angrily. "But I'll find out before I'm done."

"Why bother?" Cord rubbed a hand across his eyes, getting rid of the last of the bark and grit. "What matters is I can still walk out of here in one piece."

And, he thought grimly, whoever he'd seen up on that hillside, whoever had released the stack, would be well clear by now — or was even down among his helpers.

"You could have been killed — because of someone's stupidity." Paula Darrald dismissed the foreman with a blistering glare, then sighed apologetically. "Talos, maybe we should move on before something else happens."

Cord nodded and led the way down to the jeep. Once the girl was aboard he climbed in with a cautious care, let his back touch the seat squab, and winced as the bruised flesh made contact. He gripped the wheel and leaned forward a little.

"There's still one place on the agenda," he reminded her with a twist of a grin.

"The Sanctuary?" Paula pursed her lips. "If you really want to, there's a place about ten minutes from here where you can see what it's like. And — well, we can stop for a spell."

The last man they saw as they drove off was Elagga. The foreman stood at the track's edge and saluted solemnly as they passed, his face a picture of worried regret. But Cord glanced in the rear view mirror a moment later and saw something very different. Elagga was still staring after them, but now the regret had given place to something different, a sullen, angry scowl.

The sight was oddly pleasing, decided Cord with an odd contentment.

Somebody had decided that one Talos Cord was a nuisance, but not a dangerous nuisance — just a character who was best put out of the way for a spell. The cedar logs coming down that slope had been a fearsome sight. But though they might have broken an unpleasant quota of bones, they'd been in the lightweight rather than lethal category. Anyone who had earnestly decided he required killing would have used something much more effective than those overgrown chunks of raw fencing.

"Feeling better?" asked Paula, regarding him with a slightly puzzled air.

"Uh-huh." Being a nuisance to someone was its own justification in Field Reconnaissance's book of rules. This particular someone had been careful to wait until Paula Darrald hadn't been with him. Maybe, in fact, she'd walked back up the slope to give the plan its chance.

The idea might be an injustice to the fair-haired girl by his side. But, either way, Paula Darrald and her father required a much closer attention before he'd be prepared to decide.

★ ★ ★

High on the ridge, defying heat and rocks alike, the great club-headed guda thorn spread its shade like a welcoming bower. Beyond it, dry and sunbaked, a terrain of ragged, dark-green scrub led to the wide mouth of a valley fringed by low, harsh, broken hills. Silent, seemingly empty of life, the land brooded as if resigned to an eternal fate.

They'd stopped the jeep beside the guda thorn. Cord sat silent, frowning at the barren landscape, thinking that David Saat had been right — even a man on the run would think twice before choosing such a place.

"Not what you expected?" asked Paula quizzically.

"Not particularly." He thumbed towards the valley. "What happens if we go on?"

She shook her head. "There's a check-post just inside the valley and a warden who won't let anyone — including me — go through unless my father gives his personal okay. This is the only vehicle track leading in."

"And all this wild life he talked about?"

"There's one or two waterholes, enough for the purpose. A few antelope, smaller animals, birds, the odd lion and a couple of rhino. They've a chance here — my father's simply trying to preserve a corner for them until the average Moyallan is sensible enough to appreciate why it needs doing."

"I know what you mean," mused Cord, easing himself out from behind the steering wheel. "But if I was hungry in the bush and a hunk of fresh steak went walking by I might feel different."

She smiled slightly, reached behind her, and lifted out a small haversack. "The Sanctuary still rates as a government approved nature reserve. And in case you've any ideas, the wardens are some of the best tribal trackers in the southern district. I'd wait until you get a formal invite."

A smooth shelf of rock under the thorn's shade made a convenient table. The sandwiches were plain bread and sliced cold cuts, the coffee strong and thirst-quenching. Once they'd finished, Cord stretched out, rolled over on his stomach on the flat, hard surface, and relaxed.

Paula stayed beside him, sitting with her knees drawn up close to her chin. One hand strayed out to touch his back and he winced.

"Sorry." She eyed him strangely for a moment and seemed to be waiting. Cord turned on his side, reached out, and brought her face gently towards his. He saw her lips part softly.

Then, like the click of a shutter, the magic vanished. She shook her head, kissed him lightly on the forehead, and pulled away.

"You've had one escape already today," she said with an almost bitter touch of humour. "Let's leave it at that."

Cord sighed and lay back. "Paula . . ."

"Yes?"

"Back at the camp, what was the message you had to give Elagga?"

"That?" She flushed to the roots of her cornstraw hair and looked away from him, out towards the hills.

"Nothing important. Why?"

"I was just thinking it was lucky," he said softly. "I wouldn't have liked both of us to be in the way of that stack."

"It — It was," she agreed, then drew a deep breath. "I think it's time we started back. I've still some unpacking to do."

★ ★ ★

It was almost an hour's drive to the Darrald place, an hour in which they said little and she stayed friendly yet distant. He dropped her off at the archway gate, then turned the jeep and left.

She was still standing there when, at last, the long mimosa windbreak hid the big house from his view.

4

THE first cooking fires of the evening were beginning to smoke the sky above El Wabir when Talos Cord swung the jeep into the F.A.O. compound. It was still early enough for him to be surprised to see John Spence's pick-up truck parked beside the store sheds, but he parked the jeep alongside, left it, and moved with a painful stiffness towards the house.

"*Jambo, bwana.*" The plump houseboy was waiting to greet him at the doorway. "Bwana Spence is at work in his room, and . . . " Sildo's voice trailed away and his mouth fell open as he saw the ripped, torn state of Cord's shirt.

"A small accident," said Cord carefully. "But I'd like to wash in something bigger than a basin."

"*Ndio.*" The houseboy nodded

139

vigorously. "I will show you."

He led the way to the back of the house and stood patiently while Cord inspected the primitive cold-water shower cabinet rigged up against one wall in the open.

"Good," Cord grinned his approval. "Like to find me a towel?"

Sildo hurried off. By the time he returned and hung the towel on a nail, Cord had stripped and was already under the drenching spray. The water, lukewarm at first, soon ran like ice-cold needles and he soaped his muscular body with a sense of ultimate luxury, washing away the sweat and grime, feeling a soothing relief flow through his pores.

He came out, rough-dried, wrapped the towel around his middle, and gathered up his clothes.

"Coolin' down a wee bit, Mr Cord?" John Spence was standing a few feet away, a drink in one hand. He came nearer and inspected his guest with a detached care. "Sildo tells me you'd some kind o' an accident, but you seem in one piece. Eh . . . the jeep's all right though, isn't it?"

"Not a scratch that wasn't there before," agreed Cord, accepting the priorities. "All that happened was I got in the way of some loose timber out at Lucas Darrald's place."

"But no real harm done." It was hard to be sure whether the tall, thin Scot gained any pleasure from the fact. "Well, I suppose you could do wi' a drink."

Cord followed him into the house, dumped the clothes on the floor beside one of the armchairs, and watched while Spence made up a tumbler which was an equal mixture of whisky and water.

"Suit you?" queried Spence, handing it over.

He sipped, closed his eyes, and sighed. "Fine."

"Aye." Spence turned away and went through the ritual of locking the bottle away. "I've no time for those folk

141

who want to adulterate the stuff wi' lemonade and such nonsense." He took a long swallow from his glass. "What took you out to Darrald's part of the world?"

"Just looking around. His daughter took me on a tour."

"Paula?" One shaggy eyebrow rose in mute comment. "Then you've had a busy day, eh? I met David Saat out at one o' the farmsteads. He was telling me about that poor devil Balder, an' that he'd seen you down at the airstrip." Spence waited, saw he was going to get no particular response, and pressed harder. "No trace of the native yet, is there?"

"Not as far as I know." Cord nursed the glass between his hands. "What about you?" he demanded. "I thought you were seldom back home before dusk."

"Aye." Spence gave a sardonic grunt. "It just happens that I've some paperwork needing done. And I discovered I'm running low on cattle vaccine an' wanted to order some up before those nine-till-five desk creatures back at Nygall stopped for the night." He thumbed towards the transceiver in the corner. "When I called Headquarters on that thing the operator wanted to know if you were around."

"There's a message for me?"

"A cable of some kind." Spence crossed to the set, flicked a couple of switches, and frowned awkwardly. "I — I'll leave you to it. She'll warm up in a minute. Eh . . . all right if we eat in an hour?"

Cord nodded and grinned. "It'll give me time to get some clothes on. Look, what about later, John? I'm going in to the Mid-Con place, to meet Hal Berry. If you'd like to come . . . "

"No, thanks." Spence shifted his feet awkwardly, as if embarrassed at the use of his first name. "There's a thing or two I've got to do." The heavy eyebrows frowned in Cord's direction for another long moment. Then he swallowed the last of his drink, laid down the glass, and went away.

The armchair was pleasantly comfortable and it took an effort to leave it. But at last Cord forced himself to his feet, took a hitch at the towel at his waist, and padded across to the set. He checked there was paper and pencil handy, then picked up the microphone and got to work. The U.N. station operator at Nygall answered Spence's call-sign with a dull, bored efficiency, let a slight suggestion of interest enter his voice as Cord identified himself, then took a few seconds to locate the waiting cable.

"Here we are, El Wabir," his voice confirmed at last. "It's in code — eighteen groups. Ready?"

"Affirmative, Nygall . . . " Cord began writing as the letters came slowly over the air. As they ended, he flicked the send switch, thanked the distant operator, then tore the sheet from the message pad.

Field Reconnaissance's standard code

was a simple double-transposition affair. It took a minute or two of fairly tight concentration to work out, but when he'd finished, Cord whistled thinly through his teeth.

Andrew Beck's wordage was as usual tight and pointed.

'HAL BERRY PREVIOUS GOLD SMUGGLE SUSPECT KUWAIT. REPOSTED AS INCIDENT AVOIDANCE. NOW IMPERATIVE UPFOLLOW SUGGESTED PURCHASE DELEGATION EX-CONGO UNDESTINATION.'

He burned the message in an ashtray, carefully stirred the ashes with the pencil, then picked up his clothes and went slowly to his room. The background information on the Mid-Con man was important on its own. But the rest injected a new urgency into the situation. Cash and carry was the suggested pattern of the illegal munitions network — and if a fresh deal was currently under way then the principals would be more heavily on guard than ever.

Somewhere a considerable quantity of war material was being readied for removal. And the money involved?

It had to be big. The international rate of exchange was fairly well established . . . leaving aside such oddities as the lady in Singapore who operated a rental scheme for automatic rifles, well patronised by the more impoverished of Far East bandit society.

A rifle bullet was worth a dollar, the rifle itself up to a hundred, depending on condition. The South Africans reported a local rate of a revolver for one small uncut diamond.

But the real money was made on the major deals. There had been that shipment stopped by the French in the Mediterranean — one hundred and fifty tons of mortars and small arms. A charter flight, suspected at Shannon, seized when it refuelled at Rome, had carried six long, coffin-like wooden cases containing anti-tank guns — worth fifty thousand dollars on the market. The British were still puzzling over the destination planned for a consignment they'd found in a warehouse near Aden — two hundred machine guns, ten thousand rifles, twelve million rounds of ammunition.

And so it went on, with money, very big money, always near. If Andrew Beck was right, and it was almost sacrilege to suggest otherwise, a very large slice of somebody's loot had either arrived in the Lake Calu district or was on its way.

He took his time over changing into a clean shirt and slacks, thought for a moment, then added a dark blue silk tie from his suitcase and tied it in a neat, careful knot. When he'd finished, he inspected the result in the room's small, tarnished mirror, gave a brief grimace as he fed a handful of cheroots into his shirt pocket, and reached for his jacket.

He was all dressed up and ready to go. As long as no-one was busy scheduling another unfortunate accident, with his name on the ticket, it might be an interesting evening.

★ ★ ★

El Wabir was a dark, shapeless unreality stitched here and there by glinting lights, with the scent of wood smoke drifting on the light wind. Talos Cord drove the jeep through the deserted market-place and stopped in the broad alleyway which lay to one side of the Mid-Con building. The luminous dial of his watch read a few minutes after eight, but he wasn't the first to arrive. The jeep's headlamps shone on the white, high-sprung Mercedes station wagon from Lucas Darrald's place, parked and empty a few yards ahead.

He raised an eyebrow at the sight, switched off the jeep's lights and engine and climbed out. The ground floor of the oil company building was in darkness but upstairs was a blaze of light, with a murmur of voices coming from a partly opened window.

Somewhere around the market area a radio was blaring. In the far background, he heard shouts and laughter. The village beerhall was having a busy time.

It took a full minute's hammering on the Mid-Con door before a downstairs light switched on and Jean Berry let him in.

"Sorry," she apologised. "One of these days I'm going to make Hal fix up a bell of some kind."

"He's here?"

"He got back a couple of hours ago." Her face tightened briefly. "David Saat was waiting for him."

"About Balder being killed?" Cord nodded sympathetically. "Well, I suppose somebody has to take care of the formalities."

"Yes." Jean closed and locked the door as he came in. "I didn't have much time for old Johann. Nobody did, but — " she shook her head, forced a smile and beckoned him on. "Let's go up. As things have turned out we're having quite a gathering. Paula and her father are here."

"I saw their car." He inspected her approvingly. The daytime shirt and slacks had been exchanged for a sleeveless red dress with a scooped neckline. Her dark hair had been brushed up and back, held in place by a small, ornately carved ivory comb. "Have you had a chance to ask Hal if he'll help me?"

"Not in detail — but I told him you'd be along." She led the way through the office and up the stairway beyond. At the top she took him by the arm and guided him into the front room. "Here we are. Hal — "

Hal Berry was already crossing towards them, a big, barrel-chested man of about thirty, dark-haired like his sister but with a pudgy face, sometime broken nose and light blue eyes. Behind him, Lucas Darrald was in an armchair by the window — and

Richarn Nyeme was there too, standing with his fine-boned features twisted into a fractional smile.

"Glad to meet you, Cord." Hal Berry spoke in a gruff nasal staccato. His handclasp was tight and challenging, a heavy bronze ring on the little finger biting into Cord's flesh, the blue eyes expectant while the pressure increased.

It was an old game and one Cord had no intention of playing. He left his hand limp in the vice-like squeeze, his face expressionless.

Annoyed, the Mid-Con man persisted for a moment. Then a look of almost childish disappointment crossed his face and he gave up. Over at the window, Lucas Darrald chuckled briefly from the depths of his chair.

Berry grinned uneasily and glanced warily at his sister. Uh . . . how about getting the man a drink, Jean?"

"If the parlour tricks are over," she said frostily.

"Well then" — he flushed a little "what'll it be, Cord?" The hand wiped across the front of his white, open-necked shirt as he suggested, "How about a beer?"

"Fine," agreed Cord mildly.

"And there's one ready and waiting," said a softly amused voice from behind them. Paula Darrald stood in the doorway, a filled glass in one hand, a cigarette in the other. She was in a slim sheath of a dress, a rich dark green in colour, the silver chain at her waist — an outfit which set off her pale gold hair to perfection. "Jean, you should post public warnings about that brother of yours."

The other girl shrugged. "One day he'll grow up, I suppose."

Paula moved between them, gave Cord the glass, and looked him over with an almost clinical interest. "No signs of damage, anyway."

"Which I gather is a matter of luck as far as today is concerned," said Lucas Darrald, leaning forward a little in his chair. "Paula told me about your — ah — unfortunate moment at the lumber camp. I'm glad it was no worse."

"So am I," agreed Cord ruefully.

"We will make sure someone is punished for that carelessness," declared Nyeme, frowning over the older man's head, "but there is perhaps a lesson in it worth remembering, Mr Cord. This is a raw, sometimes still primitive part of our country and the stranger who strays too far on his own is foolish."

"I had a pretty good guide," reminded Cord.

Paula Darrald smiled a little, but with little warmth. She moved away to a table where a small pile of records lay beside a gramophone turntable.

"Jean said you wanted to see me, Cord, but that's about all." Hal Berry had found a drink of his own and was happy again. "We hadn't much chance to talk."

"She told me," nodded Cord. "Hearing about Balder must have been quite a nasty homecoming."

"These things are always bad," grunted Berry, his pudgy face showing no particular emotion. "I'll be happier when they've nailed that native. Still . . . " he glanced briefly towards Lucas Darrald. "We've had worse things happen lately. So let's talk about your survey, Cord. How long will it take you?"

"A week or so, depending how things go." Cord sipped his beer and watched a brief discussion in progress over at the record player. Jean Berry and Paula, the dark head and the fair head side by side, seemed to be having trouble in arriving at a common choice. "I'm trying to see as much of the district as I can, but I can't interfere with John Spence's work schedule."

"He is a busy man," rumbled Lucas Darrald, rising up from his chair. "Unfortunately, so am I . . . the trip I promised you into the Sanctuary will have to be postponed. Richarn had word this afternoon that we've a party of business associates arriving for a few days. Any arrangement would have to wait till they've gone."

"That's a pity," mused Cord. He fought down the interest the *Tillik Sau*'s news aroused and contented himself with what seemed a casual enough question. "When do your friends get here?"

"Tomorrow sometime."

"Flying in?"

Darrald's manner hardened. "Maybe. Or by road. Anyway, if you're only going to be here a short time it seems there's no chance of taking you to the Sanctuary."

"Perhaps it is just as well," murmured Nyeme. "After all, there is nothing in that place of possible interest to Mr Cord's people. The area is useless. That is why our government approved it as a nature reserve."

"It looked pretty barren from the glimpse I had of it," said Cord with a shrug. "You're probably right."

"If we can help in other ways, of course, just let Richarn know." Darrald gave a curt smile and raised his voice a little. "Paula, I'm going now — we'll collect you in a couple of hours."

She looked up briefly and nodded. "I'm in no hurry."

"Good." Darrald waved aside Hal Berry's move towards the door. "I know the way. Don't bother."

The small, stocky figure left the room, Nyeme close at his heels. A moment later the downstairs door banged shut. Hal Berry stayed where he was, an odd mixture of worry and something close to relief on his face. As the Mercedes started up and the station wagon growled away he gave something close to a sigh.

"This one will do." His sister's voice broke the silence. She dropped a record on the turntable, moved the pick-up arm, and a blue beat jazz number began throbbing, the volume turned low. Paula Darrald stood back, swaying slightly to the rhythm, as if she too felt some tension had been removed from the room.

"We were talking about my survey trip, Hal," murmured Cord. "One idea

I had was that an easy way to take in the country to the north-west would be if I could go along with you on a trip to the drilling sites."

The man's eyes hardened a little. "If you're thinking of the land-train, company regulations — "

"I can guess." Cord cut him short. "Only employees will be carried — the usual stuff. It just happens I'm tight for time."

"Sorry." Berry shook his head in a firm negative. "A couple of times in the past I bent the rules and got my fingers rapped by head office. Get a company authorization and you're welcome. Otherwise it's impossible."

"But, Hal . . . " his sister joined them, frowning. "Surely in the circumstances — "

"You're the one who usually waves the rulebook under my nose," he told her bluntly. "Well, this time I'm sticking by it." He glanced at Cord's glass. "Nothing personal, of course. Drink that up and I'll get you a refill."

"No thanks." Cord took the Mid-Con man's attitude calmly, knowing he couldn't be budged, deciding that something very much more than a company rulebook was on his mind. It would have been interesting to know how long Hal Berry had talked with Lucas Darrald and Nyeme beforehand — and just what had figured in the conversation. "Anyway, maybe it's time I was going. I didn't come to break up a private party."

"You're welcome to stay," protested Jean Berry. "And all I can say is that if I'd known about . . . " she threw a blistering glare in her brother's direction.

"Your temper's showing, dear," warned Paula Darrald in mock surprise. She flicked the volume of the record player up a couple of notches and drifted across the room in their general direction. "Jean, how about proving you're a friend by getting me another drink?"

The dark-haired girl drew a deep

breath and her mouth tightened. But in a moment she shrugged and turned on her heel. As she went out, her brother scowled down at his feet then sighed and went after her.

"You maybe can't help it, Talos, but trouble seems to make a habit of following you around," mused Paula Darrald at last, fingering the silver belt at her waist. Her voice became quieter, more serious. "Yet you don't look as though you'd particularly like to see people hurt. I'd say you know too much about what it can mean."

"Let's say I prefer the peaceful life — when it's possible," he said dryly. The record finished, the needle hissing on the turntable. Paula swore under her breath and stayed where she was.

"Talos, I'd like it if you remembered what Richarn said. This isn't a place where it's safe for a stranger to go wandering on his own."

"You mean people can get lost?" he asked innocently.

"Among other things." She seemed

to regret the words as soon as they left her lips, and crossed quickly to the record player. She switched it off and made a pretence of examining the other records, avoiding his gaze.

"Thanks for the warning." Cord walked slowly to the window. Outside, the night sky was bright with stars and a small group of villagers were involved in a noisy, laughing argument as they wended their way home from the beerhall. "What sort of dangers did you have in mind, Paula?"

She moistened her lips. "Just — just the obvious ones."

"The obvious what?" Jean Berry glanced at them both as she entered the room again, then went on hurriedly without waiting for a reply. "Hal's bringing the drinks. Talos, I've been talking to him but — well, maybe he's right." She drew herself a little more erect and flushed. "After all, there's every chance Mid-Con will send someone down from head office because of — well, Johann's death. It wouldn't look good if there was any irregularity about the way things were being done."

He had a vague sense of some new, invisible barrier between them, a barrier created in the few minutes she'd been gone. He noticed Paula Darrald standing very still as if she too could sense it, sense it and perhaps understand.

"Don't worry about it," he said cheerfully. "My ideas have a habit of falling to pieces — anyway, I can always fix something up with John Spence."

"I hope so." Jean Berry passed a hand almost nervously across her throat as her brother appeared, carrying a tray with four filled glasses. "And — well, Hal was wondering if you'd maybe like to do the next best thing he can offer and have a look at the land-train?"

"Right now?" The suggestion took him by surprise.

"It's as good as any other time," said Berry in his nasal staccato. He laid down the tray and screwed his pudgy face into something approaching a grin. "Call it making up a little for the other disappointment. Look, I brought another beer. How about drinking it up, then we can go straight over." He jerked his head in the direction of the two girls. "That way we give these two a chance to have a female-type gossip together."

Talos Cord rubbed a thumb slowly along his cheek then smiled and reached for the beer.

"Whenever you're ready," he agreed.

Hal Berry might have something lined up for him at the other end. But there was only one way to find out.

★ ★ ★

They left the Mid-Con building a few minutes later, Berry wearing an old wool sweater against the fast-gathering chill of the night. Outside, he turned down the alleyway and beckoned Cord on past the jeep.

"It's not far away," he explained briefly, striding on. At the end of the alley they headed to the left, past a cluster of native huts and two small, heavily shuttered shops. An askari loomed out of the darkness, pacing quietly along his beat, a rifle slung over one shoulder. The man saluted, Berry grunted a brief response, and they continued on.

A long, blank-walled building appeared ahead, surrounded by a high wire fence. Berry led the way to a wide double gate, used a key to unlock it, and swung the gate shut once they'd passed through.

He thumbed towards the building. "This is our place. I'll rouse the watchman first — but what you want to see is over on the right."

Cord peered against the darkness and picked out the strange, black silhouette which lay almost next to the warehouse. He followed Berry towards the building then slowed a little, giving a soft whistle as he had his first real glimpse of the land-train.

It was well-named and bigger, far bigger than he'd imagined.

The prime mover was a massive six-wheeled tractor unit fitted with balloon tyres which were each the height of a man. An enclosed cab was set above, with a long extension to the rear. Behind the tractor, hitched one to the other by stout metal towbars, linked by hydraulic brake cables and electrical harness, three long balloon-tyred trailers were coupled together like so many empty railway flat-cars.

Berry knocked on the warehouse door. It opened, throwing a dull pool of light from within. An overalled figure appeared briefly, framed in the glow, there was a short, low-voiced conversation, and the door closed again. Next moment, a row of powerful arc lamps poured their white glare from the warehouse roof, bathing the yard in their light.

Hands in his pockets, Hal Berry came back with a slight swagger in his walk.

"Well, what do you think of her?" he demanded.

"Quite a rig," admitted Cord, fascinated at the powerful monster now exposed in all its detail of travel-stained steel framework, massive, grimy radiator and funnel-like twin exhausts.

"As good as they come," declared Berry, a genuine pride in his nasal tones. "The engine's a double-banked sixteen cylinder diesel — she'll pull a forty thousand pound payload."

"What range?"

"On the regular tanks, three hundred miles at around fifteen miles an hour. But I carry another two hundred miles in reserve."

"And how many of a crew?" Cord moved closer, sniffing the pungent scent of oil still coming from the tractor's engine, noting the swivel-mounted spotlight on its roof and massive treads built into each tyre.

"Crew?" Berry laughed and spat expressively. "I'm on my own as far as driving's concerned — I prefer it.

Usually I take a couple of native boys along to handle the chores, but that's it."

He swung himself up the three metal steps which led to the high cab, opened the door, eased himself in, and waited for Cord to follow. Inside was remarkably like being on the bridge of a yacht — an illusion heightened by the heavy brass compass mounted next to the king-sized steering wheel. The long bench seat running the width of the cab would have held four men with room to spare.

"I've seen some heavy transports, but this beats them all," murmured Cord appreciatively. "And you cover some pretty rugged country with her, from what I've heard."

"She can cope." Berry tapped the club-like gear lever with one stubby forefinger. "Counting secondary drive I've a sixteen-speed box — power to all six wheels when it's needed." He reached out, released the big handbrake, and tugged it on again with a hiss of air from a master cylinder. "Servoassisted hydraulics, power steering, self-sealing tyres — the design is Mid-Con, but the original idea was a U.S. Army logistic cargo carrier project."

"What's in behind?" asked Cord, thumbing at the hatch set in the bulkhead at the back of the seats.

"Crew quarters for myself — a bunk, that sort of thing." Berry slid the hatch open a few inches and let him see the interior of the spartan compartment. He nodded towards a shotgun held in clips to one side of the bunk. "Now and again I get a chance to collect some fresh meat for supper."

"All home comforts," said Cord dryly. As the hatch slid shut again he cleared his throat in gentle fashion. "What about the contract labour workers?"

"Eh?" The Mid-Con man was immediately on his guard. "What about them?"

Cord shrugged. "Jean mentioned you ferry them occasionally — that some on their way home were killed in the plane crash. I wondered if you hitched on an extra trailer when you were carrying a squad or — well, what happened."

"They ride on the flat-trucks," grunted Berry. He fumbled in the pockets of his slacks, found his cigarettes, and lit one carefully. "There's no need for anything more."

"Will there be any men going out with the next load?" He saw the man's eyes narrow and quickly explained, "I'm interested in where their homes are located — it could be useful in my report."

"Then you're out of luck. The next is a routine supply run." Berry smoked in silence for a moment then eased out from behind the wheel. "Here, I'll show you what we'll carry — and the warehouse itself. Then you've seen the lot."

They climbed down from the cab, walked across the yard, and entered the building. The main overhead lights were already burning and the watchman, a young, muscular Moyallan with a thick, woolly mop of black, well-greased hair, came forward. A short, heavy baton hung from a leather belt at his waist, balanced on the other hip by a clip holding a large rubber torch.

"*Bwana?*"

"*Hapana . . . endelea . . .* " Berry waved him aside, led Cord a little way across the concrete floor, then gestured around. "There you are — Aladdin's cave, Mid-Con style."

Long sections of metal piping, crated engine spares, boxed equipment, cases and cartons of tinned food, drums of fuel — the great hanger-like space was filled in neatly galleried order. Brought by lorry from the coast, stock-piled at El Wabir till the land-train was ordered to move them on the final stage of their journey, the tons of stores held for the drilling camps covered most conceivable needs and eventualities.

"There's a lot of value in this stuff," mused Cord. "Had any trouble from pilferers?"

"None." Berry grinned and jerked his head in the direction of the watchman. "Our boy was hand-picked for the job. When there's a local celebration and he's togged up in his tribal stuff he sticks a couple of ostrich feathers in his hair. Around here each feather means a man killed, hand-to-hand style." His blue eyes regarded Cord keenly for a moment, then he beckoned him to follow. "Walk down here and you'll find our grocery section. They eat well at the drilling camps."

They moved down the galleries, footsteps echoing, Berry stopping every now and again to identify an item or explain a need. At last, gradually, he led Cord back towards the main door then came to a sudden halt.

"Look, there's another reason why I don't want passengers right now — one I don't want Jean to know about. Okay?"

"I'd like to hear it," said Cord cautiously.

"All right. A bunch of *shifta* were

spotted not far from the drilling rigs last week. It's a small gang as far as we know, one that has strayed in from the west an' is starting to make a nuisance in the area — wild boys who shoot first then quarrel about who should own your boots. They've probably never heard of the U.N. and if you told them they wouldn't be impressed." Berry smacked fist against palm in almost theatrical emphasis. "I'm trying to say that apart from anything else it's too risky right now."

Cord decided to be awkward. "You've been all right so far — "

The other man growled impatiently. "Look, if I did get shot up I'd draw a pension — or Jean would. If you get shot up at the same ruddy time an' no authorization from head office for you being along, my pension would go out of the window. Understand?"

"It's a good argument," admitted Cord. It was, he had to admit to himself, a better one than he'd have expected from the man, probably too good to be all his own work. Except that David Saat would have been outraged at the suggestion such a *shifta* gang could be anywhere near without his knowing.

"Then it's settled." Berry made no secret of his relief. "How about going back to the house now?"

Cord glanced at his watch then shook his head with the air of a man with a wearisome task ahead. "It's late — I think I'll just head back to Spence's compound. I promised him we'd look through some statistics tonight."

"Suit yourself," shrugged Berry. "If that's what you want to do then I'll maybe stay here for a spell and catch up on some work of my own. Think you can find your own way to the jeep?"

"I'll manage."

"Fine." The Mid-Con man steered him towards the door. "Maybe once I get back from this next run I can wangle some time off an' show you around a little."

Cord nodded his thanks and left, the watchman padding a few paces ahead, holding the fence gate open till he was outside, then carefully closing it behind him. As the man headed back towards the building Cord fished a cheroot from his shirt pocket, bit the end, and lit it with a thoughtful deliberation.

The warehouse door closed and a moment later the floodlamps flickered out, leaving the yard in darkness. Cord swore softly to himself. He'd take a bet of a year's pay against a half-acre of Lake Calu's scrubland that Hal Berry was helping in something much less innocent than a glorified trucking operation. And, though the odds might be longer, he'd have bet still more that Lucas Darrald's arriving 'business associates' were very likely a party of militant-minded Congolese politicos, out on a shopping trip to buy an edge of steel for their next piece of hell-raising.

Bombs and bullets . . . he clenched the cheroot almost angrily between his teeth, drew on it until the tip glowed cherry-red in the night, and strode off down the narrow village street.

The jeep was easy enough to locate. He climbed aboard, started it, reversed quietly out of the alley, and drove out of El Wabir in the direction of the airstrip. If anything was happening out there, he might as well barge into the party.

Headlamps blazing, the jeep reached the *ban* grass stretch, bumped across, then steadied as its wheels met the wire mesh runway. The twin beams of light swung across the darkness, picked out Darrald's twin-engined plane parked at its usual place, then, as they lit the office hut beyond, showed a solitary figure waiting on its verandah.

Cord slowed as he recognised the askari's uniform. Rifle at the ready, the man stood warily until he'd stopped alongside then relaxed and gave a grin of recognition.

"*Jambo, bwana!*" The rifle went back on its sling over the askari's shoulder.

"You look for Inspector Saat?"

"*Hapana*." Cord shook his head. "I came to find out if any aircraft had landed."

"Aeroplanes . . . here, at night?" The man gave a puzzled frown. "No, *bwana*. I stay here in case that *mtundu* Wani should return."

"Had any other visitors?" Cord drew another of the cheroots from his pocket and handed it across.

"*Ndio*," nodded the askari, sniffing the tobacco with an appreciative grin. "A little while back. The *Tillik Sau* comes to look at his aeroplane. He went inside it, then drove away again."

"With Nyeme?"

The man nodded, then leaned back against the hut, struck a match, and lit his new-found prize. Cord gave him a brief wave of thanks, slid the jeep into gear, and drove back across the strip at a gentle pace. By the time he'd reached the edge of El Wabir his mind was made up. As long as David Saat was keeping even a nominal eye on the landing ground it was unlikely to figure in Darrald's plans concerning those visiting 'business associates'. If the discovery had upset Darrald's scheduled plan and he'd used the aircraft's radio to pass the word, then there seemed one other possibility open to him.

A little way on, Cord drew the jeep into the patch of shadow between two cinder-block buildings, switched off lights and engine, and started walking through the quiet village. A drunk sprawled mumbling in a doorway was the only life in sight — El Wabir was early enough in settling down to sleep. He reached the market-place, took his bearings from the Mid-Con building, and moved on more cautiously towards the warehouse.

A dump of rusty oil drums made a handy shelter not far from the fenced-off yard. He got behind them as something small and long-tailed scurried away from close by his feet, and gave a murmur of grim satisfaction

176

as the moonlight showed the pale shape of the Mercedes station wagon parked without lights inside the wire.

Close on fifteen minutes passed by his watch before the warehouse door opened. Hal Berry was first to emerge from the brightly lit doorway, followed quickly by Lucas Darrald and Nyeme. They exchanged brief farewells, and Berry hurried across to open the fence gate while the other men boarded the station wagon.

Cord shrank back as the vehicle left the yard and, headlights beaming, drove close past his shelter. Then, as the red-tail-lamps disappeared along the village, he saw Berry close the gate and return to the warehouse.

The temptation was strong to stay where he was, wait until Berry would leave, then get over that fence. But there would still be the watchman, still the chance of his thin but apparently intact cover story being broken.

Reluctantly, he left his hiding-place and walked back towards the jeep.

For now, he might as well return to John Spence's company — Food and Agriculture officials had no business being out too late at night.

* * *

Once clear of the village, the jeep bumped happily along the track which snaked through the scrubland to Spence's compound. Talos Cord drove steadily, his mind busy on what he should do next. He was beginning to need help, need it badly if he was to keep tabs on all that might happen. David Saat and his askaris were one obvious solution — yet Andrew Beck took a poor view of his Field Reconnaissance men embroiling outsiders in their work until a cut and dried situation required attention. Even then, the direct approach wasn't encouraged.

That left Spence, if the local U.N. agent could be persuaded that the United Nations' ideals of brotherly peace sometimes had to be achieved by a spot of unbrotherly action. He frowned at the problem, let the jeep's speedometer needle drop a little under the 'thirty' mark as the track took a slow curve between two small scrub-covered knolls, then suddenly swung the wheel and tried to jam on the foot-brake.

It was too late. The rope had jerked up across the track when he was less than five yards distant. There was only time to try to throw himself sideways from behind the steering wheel, for his hands to make an instinctive attempt to shield his face.

The ambush had been neatly gauged. One moment the taut rope brushed along the jeep's bonnet, the next it met the slender windscreen — and the world swung with a shatter of glass, a squeal of tyre rubber, and a final rip of buckled, twisted metal as the little vehicle swayed and jerked with the impact, broke the rope, then crashed over on its side. Catapulted out of the seat, Cord smashed down into a tough, unyielding patch of viciously hooked thornbush which ripped and clawed at his limbs as he tried to drag himself clear. At the side of the track, the jeep's horn blared as a wire shorted — blared and kept on, a high-pitched tortured note with no ending.

Two dark shapes were moving across the shrub, heading in his direction, moving quickly, yet obviously still uncertain as to where he lay. He heaved again, felt the thorns rip afresh, then broke loose. A cry signalled that he'd been seen and a moment later the two men rushed towards him.

He sidestepped the first figure, saw the heavy club in the other man's hand start to swing, and hurled himself to one side. As he hit the ground, rolling, picking himself up fast, both men came on again. This time the man with the club was first — and as the horn's strident note wailed on he saw the second gripped a rifle.

But that first chance had made the difference, the seconds between being a mere cornered, fighting animal and now still cornered, still fighting, but with a mind which merged savage instinct with cold, disciplined judgement.

The man with the club, heavy and thick-shouldered, charged first. Cord gauged his moment, threw himself back, and, as his shoulders hit the ground, swung his right leg high in a stiff, fast arc. The heel of his moccasin took the man in the pit of the stomach with a noise like a mallet hitting butter. The attacker star-fished back with a scream — and Cord was already rolling as the other man lunged his rifle butt in infantry style, aiming at Cord's head.

It missed, the steel butt-plate sparked against a stone as it hammered against the ground — and Cord was clear, scrambling to his feet again. Somewhere in the background the first man was coughing and staggering towards them again — but for the moment he could be ignored, just as the din from the jeep's horn could be ignored as part of the background nightmare.

This time the rifleman was more careful. He moved nearer at a slow crouch, a tall, thin man, his body, naked except for a ragged pair of shorts, a dark, ebony menace which somehow glistened in the moonlight. Gradually, he forced Cord back a step at a time — and the inevitable happened, a stray root of thornbrush sent Cord sprawling backwards, crashing into its branches.

The rifle swung, the butt landed a numbing blow high on Cord's left arm. But the bush had still broken the force, its thorns gripped the rifle's sling, and for a few brief seconds its wielder was helpless.

It was the kind of chance which seldom comes twice. As the man wrenched free and pulled back Cord hurtled forward. His two hands gripped the rifle's length as a circus artist might use a trapeze bar, his whole body swung up, and his knees took the other man hard on the body. They went down together, the rifle clattering to one side, Cord's hands slipping as he tried in vain to get some grip on the carefully oiled body.

He changed his tactics, left hand searching up to grip hard on the thick, greasy hair, grip, twist and hold on while the man beneath him fought and heaved. A heavy fist slammed against his face, the man's breath was hot in his nostrils — then a sudden triumph in the snarling face so close to his own gave its own warning. Cord let go, trying to roll clear.

The first attacker was behind him, club raised. But the blow didn't fall. Two harsh headlamp beams were sweeping towards them, a moment later the roar of a vehicle's engine penetrated above the din of the jeep's horn, then the Land-Rover was skidding to a halt only yards away, its doors flying open.

One of the men cried out, the other answered, Cord was ignored in their sudden scramble — and they were running into the darkness while booted feet pounded towards him.

First to arrive, David Saat came

to a halt, his voice sounding like a bull-horn as he ordered the fleeing pair to stop. Their only reply was a hasty rifle-shot from somewhere in the scrub, and the policeman answered it in turn with a coughing blast of fire from his Sterling gun.

"What the hell's happening?" John Spence was beside Cord, helping him to his feet, a look of shock and anger on his face. Cord clung to him for a moment, breathless, while Saat fired a second, shorter spray of bullets into the night.

"Nice — nice to see you." Cord moistened his dry lips, managed a grin, and pulled himself upright. "You're just in time."

"We heard that damned horn." Spence glared round at the overturned jeep, marched purposefully towards it, and a moment later the blare died. The silence was a relief on its own. He came back, and stared at Cord again. "I should have known — man, what the hell are you up to around here?"

Saat was a few paces away, his thick-featured face a hard mask in the Land-Rover's lights, the Sterling gun still ready at his hip. He gave a brief rumble of agreement. "I am going to ask the same. But not here. Not when there is someone out there with a gun and a possible urge to use it."

Spence nodded. "Then let's get back to the compound. And then, Cord, we're going to talk."

"That's what I had in mind," agreed Cord wearily.

"Even before this happened, Mr Cord?" demanded Saat with an acid sarcasm.

"Even before," agreed Cord. He gazed ruefully at his ripped clothing. "I'll say this for your country, Inspector. It's no place for a man who likes to call himself a peacemaker!"

5

AT the F.A.O. compound, Spence's plump houseboy gave a grin of nervous relief as the Land-Rover stopped and its three occupants climbed out.

"I heard shooting, *bwana*" — he had an old shotgun cradled awkwardly in his arms.

"It's finished, Sildo," growled Spence. "Put that damned thing away before you blow your fool head off."

"*Ndio.*" The houseboy nodded thankfully. "You want coffee or something maybe?"

"Aye it would help," agreed his employer. He beckoned Cord and Saat to follow him, led the way into the house, and waved them into chairs. But he remained where he was, a tall, stooped figure, sucking on his unlit pipe as he scowled down at his returned houseguest.

"Well, Mr Cord?"

"Perhaps we should give him a chance to rest for a little — " began Saat.

"And a chance to think up some tall story?" Spence sniffed derisively. "No. Not this time."

Cord sighed and rubbed a hand along the smooth, worn leather of his armchair. "I don't mind. And I'm glad you showed up."

"You were lucky," said Spence grimly.

"Very lucky," nodded David Saat. He made a leisurely job of unbuttoning his uniform jacket and relaxed with a sigh. "I was here with John, waiting your return, when we heard the sound of that horn — heard it, and came quickly."

"Mind telling me why you were wanting to see me?" asked Cord, immediately curious.

"There is no hurry about it," declared the policeman softly. "For the moment,

I would rather listen to you."

"And let's forget the nonsense about you being on this agricultural survey," added Spence with a heavy sarcasm. "I've played along wi' that till now, but not any more."

Cord raised an apologetic eyebrow. "Was it so obvious?"

"To me. If you do this kind o' thing regularly take a bit more care over your homework. Remember we talked about cotton when I was showin' you round?" The Scot's mouth twisted in disgust. "I tried you out — an' you made mistakes anyone wi' the slightest knowledge would have avoided. The Moyallan cotton strain happens to have a red flower. Yellow is the colour o' the Egyptian strain we're bringing in."

"I'll remember. I had to come here in — well, rather a rush." Cord leaned forward and smiled, though the ache in his shoulder was still pounding. "Then I suppose you checked with your director at Nygall?"

"Aye, and was told to mind my own

business." Spence drew an indignant breath. "Only I happen to believe what happens in my district is very much my business."

"It is my district too," murmured Saat. The squat, burly Moyallan slouched deeper in his chair, hands in his pockets. "My own checking was necessarily a little more discreet because of things Mr Cord had already admitted to me. As he warned me, I found my superiors feel that particularly at this time there could be political embarrassment involved in his presence. They are most curious about why he is here." He chuckled calmly. "We are — well, sensitive about such things."

"I know how I feel — " Spence broke off with a growl as Sildo padded into the room carrying a laden tray. The houseboy served the coffee, offered sugar and cream, gave Cord a quick, sympathetic smile, then returned to his kitchen.

David Saat sipped his cup and smacked his thick lips approvingly.

"*Vizuri* . . . and now, Mr Cord, it is your turn. You say you will tell us what you are doing. One reason for this change, I suppose, must be that you need our help."

Cord hesitated, shrugged, and nodded. "As things stand, yes."

Spence sniffed, but the policeman was interested. "And your authority for seeking this help?"

"Here and for the moment, just words." Cord knew this was where he might fall flat, but hoped for the best. "They're part of the U.N. charter . . . 'to ensure by the institution of methods, that armed force shall not be used save in the common interest'."

"So. And you are one of these 'instituted methods'?" Saat's quiet eyes twinkled briefly. "Go on, please."

Cord glanced at John Spence, still standing, now slowly and almost pugnaciously stuffing tobacco into the bowl of his pipe. "Maybe you should sit down. This will take time."

"I'll stand if I choose. And you

missed out a bit in that handy little quote, Cord — a bit about 'the acceptance of principle'."

"Stop acting like a five-year-old, John," said Saat with a sudden, sharp authority. "Sit down and give him a chance."

Reluctantly, Spence obeyed, sitting down gingerly, very straight, his feet together.

"Begin with a fact, the only one hundred per cent fact I've got." Cord's voice fell to a quiet, business-like tone which held its own underlying emphasis. "Begin with a dead man whose name was Robert Tollogo . . ."

In the same quiet, unemotional manner he talked on for a full ten minutes, telling them what he knew, outlining possibilities, admitting weaknesses. After the first minute David Saat laid down his cup and let it lie forgotten. From frank incredulity, Spence's expression gradually changed to a frowning, doubtful uncertainty.

When Cord finished, Saat gnawed

his lip unhappily. "Do you realise just what it means if all this is true? Lucas Darrald is a man who — "

"Who carries a lot of weight," nodded Cord. "Does it worry you?"

"I would be a fool to deny it." Saat chose his words with care. "As for the man himself — he has friends, he is not like some whites who still think of us as just down from the trees. He treats us as equals, as a man must who wishes to prosper in business. But *nani afahauye* . . . who knows? It is always hard to judge a man who has power."

They sat silent for a long moment. Somewhere outside a cricket broke off singing then started again on the same throbbing note. Spence squirmed in his chair, struck a match and puffed on his pipe. When he spoke, he was on the defensive. "Even if we accepted all this, Cord, you can't brand a man a gun-runner on the strength of possibilities."

"Gun-runner?" Cord treated the word with contempt. "I'm talking about a different kind of league. If our Field Reconnaissance reports are right, then this particular outfit supply wars, made-to-measure."

"And I have seen what that can mean. A war in this part of the world has a brutality all its own." David Saat half-closed his eyes, as if to shut out the memory. "I would rather not say where or when or why I was involved — a young man can be foolish, then find it too late for regrets. But I want no more of such things." He rose to his feet, one hand going into his jacket pocket. "I will help you — and there is a practical enough reason why I should, the one which brought me here tonight."

The little package hit the surface of the table between them. Cord picked it up, removed the cloth wrapping, and stared down at a small tin box.

"Open it," invited the Moyallan. "One of my askaris found it buried under the earth floor of the man Wani's hut. His wife says he did not know it was there — I think we can believe her."

Cord eased open the lid and gave a whistle of surprise as he smoothed out the wedge of banknotes which had nestled within.

"Two hundred dollars," said Saat quietly. "More money than most men around Lake Calu could save in a lifetime. And the bills have not been long buried. Even in that tin, they would have been damaged by termites before long."

"So where did he get it and why did he leave it behind?" Cord folded the money again and returned it to the box. "Maybe it was his share for keeping quiet about the airstrip log being altered — "

"And maybe he didn't come back for it because he was killed, like Balder?" John Spence's thin, weary face was strained, his voice struggling for the correct blend of dignity and apology. "I came out here to help people. I — I'm damned if that just means going around talking, handing out, or sticking hypodermic needles in beasts'

194

backsides." He straightened up, his decision made. "Mr Cord, you'll take a whisky — a large one."

Cord smiled a little and nodded. Spence marched across to the desk, unlocked it, poured three stiff measures from his treasured bottle, and brought the glasses to the table. As the others joined him, the Scot raised his drink in a brief, silent toast, took a long swallow, then wiped his lips with the back of his hand and gave a long, committed sigh.

"Well, what do we do?" he demanded.

"That rather depends on one question," murmured Saat. "How many people know that our friend Talos is not what he has — ah — tried to appear?"

"I've said nothing," declared Spence.

"I think it's still moderately watertight," said Cord slowly. "Tonight's business was on the same pattern as the log-rolling trick. One of that pair of imitation *shifta* had a rifle, and handled it like an expert. They could have killed me the easy way — but their orders may have been restricted to beating me up, making it look like a robbery. Then I'd be out of circulation for a spell, but there'd be no great rumpus."

"Unfortunately, that would be true," admitted Saat. He rubbed his chin thoughtfully. "All this, yet how was it that the *Tillik Sau*'s son died in the same plane as your friend Tollogo?"

"Somebody's mistake — may be his father's," shrugged Cord grimly. "Can you set up a watch on Berry at the Mid-Con warehouse?"

"With little trouble." Saat grinned. "One of my men is friendly with a young woman whose hut is nearby. And the watch at the airstrip?"

"I'd keep it going. Is there anywhere else around here a plane could touch down?"

Saat and Spence exchanged glances. Spence shook his head. "Not without a lot of preparation."

"Good. Now you, John. Know any

good poacher, the kind who might risk sneaking into Darrald's nature reserve now and again? A man you can trust?"

The Scot's thin face crinkled in the makings of a smile. "You ask me that with the district inspector of police right next to us?"

"Suddenly, I have gone deaf," Saat told him solemnly.

"Then there's one," nodded Spence. "You've already met him — Kalloe, the fellows who got that load of cotton seed. He — eh — " he glanced at Saat and chuckled — "he never seems short of meat. The Sanctuary isn't a place many of them would go near, because Darrald's game wardens are notoriously trigger-happy. But I think he takes the chance. You want to talk to him?"

"I want him as a guide," said Cord. "For sometime tomorrow. I want to get into that place, see what I can, and get out again in one piece."

"I would give no guarantees." Saat's broad face was suddenly serious again. "Perhaps I could arrange some necessary, official visit — a search for the man Wani, for instance."

Cord shook his head. "They'd be ready for you, one way or another." He finished his drink and laid down the glass. "Until we've more proof we've got to treat this like walking on eggs. That means going gently, or it becomes messy."

"There's — well, one thing that's still difficult to believe." John Spence cleared his throat awkwardly. "I've never had much time for Hal Berry, but his sister is a decent young woman." He stopped hopefully, saw Cord was simply waiting, and went on with an uneasy determination. "Do either of these girls have to be involved?"

Cord shrugged. "All I know is they're both hiding something, maybe different things for different reasons. I'm not sitting as judge and jury on anyone, John." He deliberately steered away from it. "Earlier on, Jean did show me that Tollogo was on the Mid-Con list as a cook-boy at their number five drill site. Whether he ever got there is another matter."

"I have a sergeant, a good man, who could drive there and back in a day," said Saat, glancing at his watch. "I will arrange it." He began to fasten his jacket, a slow smile on his face. "There is not much more we can do tonight. But tomorrow — I think we will have a busy enough time."

They said goodnight, he picked up his cap, and Spence saw him out. The Scot returned as the Land-Rover pulled away.

Cord yawned. The pain in his shoulder had faded, but he felt a strong and growing need for sleep. He yawned again, and looked up to find Spence standing over him.

"Away to your bed, man." The voice was brusque, but trying hard to be friendly. "I'll stay up for a spell longer — that bottle o' mine is all the company I'll need this night."

★ ★ ★

Cord was asleep the moment his head hit the pillow. He knew nothing more until a hand was gently shaking his shoulder, shaking and refusing to stop at his mumbled protests. At last he forced one eye open, squinted up, and met the houseboy's grinning face. The room was bathed in a glare of warm sunlight, the diesel generator was humming, and his mouth tasted like an abandoned glue factory.

"Tea, *bwana*." Sildo pointed to the cup beside the bed. "Maybe you get up now, eh?"

He glanced at his watch and groaned. It was past 1 a.m., the day was well begun, and time had been wasting. "Where's Bwana Spence, Sildo?"

"Out." The houseboy spread his hands in apology. "All he tells me is to wake you at this time, and that I have to say he will be back once he has arranged certain things."

"Right." Cord swallowed some of the scalding tea, peeled back the thin bedsheet and blanket, and yawned himself fully awake. "No more trouble overnight?"

"No — which filled me with thankfulness." Sildo went out, closing the door, still shaking his head. Cord grinned then winced as he got his feet and stretched. The bruise on his shoulder where the rifle butt had struck was a livid purple — still, he consoled himself, it would have been a worse story if the blow had connected in the way it was intended.

Washed, shaved, and dressed, he went through, ate the breakfast Sildo had waiting, then lit a cheroot and crossed over to the window.

The view was to the south-west, towards El Wabir and Lake Calu — dull, parched, monotony, hot and dusty, so much tall *ban* grass and scrub. Yet there had been more than a touch of insistent pride in John Spence's voice when he'd called it 'my district'. He'd heard it said that Food and Agriculture men were chosen for their obstinacy. Out here it was a quality which had to be respected — respected as much as the difficulties that waited them.

A glint of sunlight reflected from a metal roof brought his attention back to the track from the village. In a moment, the flash came again, nearer, and he could see the dust cloud stirred up by the approaching vehicle. He grinned and headed for the door. If this was Spence already, the tall, thin Scot must have been quickly persuasive when it came to organising his promised guide.

But it wasn't the Ford utility which came into view a few moments later. Cord frowned as an old red Packard saloon drew nearer, then swore softly as it halted by the compound gateway and he recognised the figure behind the dusty windscreen.

"Morning — " Jean Berry leaned out of the opened driver's window, a hesitant smile on her face, a pair of dark sun-glasses hiding her eyes.

"Hello, Jean." He walked over to the car and greeted her with a cheerful nod. "Sorry I didn't show up again last night. How'd the rest of your get-together turn out?"

"All right." She pursed her lips for a moment. "Better than what happened to you — I passed what's left of the jeep on the way up."

"Two local lads with ambitions and a handy length of rope," he said ruefully.

The girl nodded. She was back in shirt and jeans again, and an old wide-brimmed hat lay on the seat beside her. "I heard. John Spence looked in earlier — we carry a stock of jeep spares. How do you feel?"

"Fine — but in no mood for another dose of the same," he admitted, rubbing a hand across his chin. "Like to come into the house for a spell?"

"No, I can't stay long." The dark-haired girl removed the sunglasses and stared at him hopefully. "Talos, Hal and I had another talk last night about — well, about your wanting to see the drilling sites."

He shrugged, leaned against the

metal of the car, then drew back again quickly as he felt its temperature. "Nothing to worry about — I'll fix up something."

"Maybe you won't need to. I've some time off due to me and this is our own car. If I like to take you on a trip — "

"You?"

She flushed a little and ran her tongue over her lips. "I've done the trip with Hal, I know the route. There'd be nothing to worry about."

"Wouldn't there?" he eyed her quizzically. "You're sure your brother knows about this? Last night he spun me a long story about some bunch of *shiftas* roaming out there — "

"He was just trying to make a better job of saying 'no'. It's safe enough, and two days would do it. If we left this afternoon, early, we could probably reach the first drill site by dusk."

"I see." It made sense now. Two days away from the area, two days when he wouldn't be around to annoy anyone.

A different style of tactic, a different kind of bait — he scratched his head apologetically. "Sorry, Jean, it's a good idea but I've already organised a work schedule for the next couple of days, made arrangements. Maybe after that we could do it — I like the idea."

"But this would give you the chance you wanted," she protested.

"It's just one of these things," he said with an apologetic shrug. "I've got a heavy programme to get through and not long to do it in."

"I see." Her voice dulled and a look which was somehow strained and almost fearful came into her eyes. "Well, I — that's it, I suppose."

"Jean . . . " he laid a hand on her arm. "Like to talk about it?"

Her head jerked up. "About what?"

"Just whatever's got you worried." He gave a lop-sided grin of reassurance. "Look, I represent a fairly king-sized organisation. There's more than a chance I could help."

The girl looked at him, shook her

head, and reached forward to start the engine.

"Hold on," protested Cord as it fired to life. "There's one favour you could do for me — give me a lift down to the jeep. I'd like to see it for myself in broad daylight."

"Get in," she said briefly, blipping the accelerator with her foot. He went round, opened the passenger door, and was still swinging himself aboard when she slammed the car into gear and it jerked forward.

"Hey, what's the hurry?" he protested as he slammed the door and clung to the seat.

"Hurry?" Her hands were knuckle-white on the steering wheel and she didn't take her eyes from the road. "You're not the only one with a heavy programme."

"That's all?"

She didn't answer. The car swept down to the twin knolls, bounced to a halt just short of the wide skid-marks and the overturned jeep, and Cord reached for the door.

"Talos . . . "

"Uh-huh?" Cord waited, his face calm, his manner encouraging.

"Just — " she bit her lip. "Just if you change your mind let me know."

"I'll remember." He got out, closed the door, saw her eyes on him again in that same strange way, then the car was driving off, dust spinning from its wheels.

As it vanished down the track, Cord turned his attention to the jeep. It still lay on its side, the windscreen smashed, bodywork twisted. One of the front tyres was flat, the steering wheel spun lazily when he tried it, and a pool of oil had seeped from the sump on to the dry earth beneath. He patted the bonnet ruefully and moved to the broken rope. One end had been firmly anchored to a finger-shaped outcrop of rock, the other had been pulled tight round the thick base of a deep-rooted thornbush.

There was the place where he'd been

thrown — a scrap of cloth from his shirt still clinging to a branch. He took a couple of steps nearer, stopped, frowned, then bent down and picked up the dark, cylinder-like object lying half-hidden beneath the scrub. The heavy rubber torch still worked, only the metal belt-clip at its base was broken. Cord thumped it thoughtfully against the palm of his other hand. The last time he'd seen this torch — or its twin — it had been swinging from the belt of Hal Berry's night guard at the Mid-Con warehouse.

The sound of an approaching engine made him turn, and he moved out to the edge of the track as John Spence's blue Ford utility swayed into sight. The soot was alone behind the wheel, and there was a frown on his face as he pulled up and Cord climbed aboard.

"I was out o' luck," said Spence brusquely. "Sorry — but that damned Kalloe won't do it. Says he hasn't been near the Sanctuary for over a year and doesn't have any intention of going back."

"Scared?" Cord closed the door and settled back against the worn upholstery. "Maybe if the price was right — "

"I tried that," growled Spence, putting the utility into gear again. "He's just not interested, and he showed me why. The last time he went up there he had to have a bullet dug out of his leg, and at that he reckons he was lucky. Anyway, he says, no poacher would want to waste time up there even if things were different."

"Why?"

Spence swore as they hit a pothole. "It doesn't make sense to me. He says the animals have all gone from there, so why bother!"

"In a so-called nature reserve." Cord drew a deep breath, knowing a sudden eager curiosity. "Look, John, that could mean several things on its own."

The compound lay ahead. Spence steered the utility in through the gate, switched off the engine, and nodded. "Thought you might feel that way, man." A slow smile filtered across his thin face. "That's why I got him to help me draw a wee map, an' — well, I think the word is 'pumped' anything I could out o' him. David Saat is taking care of things in El Wabir like we arranged and I've told him about this, so if you just give me time to fill up on fuel we — "

"We?" Cord's eyes narrowed, then he shook his head. "I get paid for this sort of thing — you don't."

"But it's my district," declared Spence with a stubborn emphasis.

"Suppose . . . " Cord hesitated, and put a compromise with as much tact as he could. "John, there's no dividend in us both going in and maybe both ending up in the bag. But I'd agree it might make sense if I went in knowing that you weren't too far away."

"What do you mean by 'not too far'?" Spence was immediately suspicious.

"Somewhere handy in the background,

with a rifle if you've got one."

"Aye." Spence scowled but grudgingly agreed. "Well, we'll get nowhere staying here on our backsides. Let's get ready."

★ ★ ★

They were ready within the hour. John Spence refuelled the utility, loaded aboard a couple of rifles and some other gear, then disappeared for a spell to emerge with a small, paper-wrapped package which he thrust quickly under the Ford's seat. Cord's preparations were less involved, but when he came out, ready to leave, a coded cable was on its way via Nygall to Andrew Beck's office in New York — and the black metal box in his suitcase was empty. The Neuhausen automatic was in the right-hand pocket of his fawn, zip-fastened jerkin and three spare clips of its fat, deadly 9 mm Parabellum cartridges bulged the left.

Maybe he wouldn't have to use it.

But if he did, then it was a work-tool which he knew like an old friend. He'd had it a long time, ever since Andrew Beck had made it a twenty-first birthday gift.

Spence was already behind the wheel, openly impatient to begin the journey. Cord swung into the passenger seat, smiled, and nodded.

"Right . . . " Spence waved a hand in farewell to Sildo, who was standing by the house door. The starter whirred, the engine roared, and they were on their way.

The map, such as it was, had been scrawled on the back of an F.A.O. receipt form. Cord carried it on his knee, but his driver seemed in no doubt about their route.

"From here we go west, shading north west, for quite a spell," he said, raising his voice above the utility's growl. "What you saw on that trip with Paula Darrald was the Sanctuary's front door. We're going round to the tradesmen's entrance."

"How far?"

"Till we get there?" Spence shrugged. "I reckon a shade over forty miles. Then we go on foot for a couple of miles, heading south, with a reasonable amount o' cover. After that . . . " his eyes showed their perplexity " . . . well, there's about a hundred square miles o' broken ground, hills and the rest."

"Ten by ten," murmured Cord. "It sounds easier that way."

"Aye." The man grinned and fed a little more accelerator as the track ahead levelled for a spell. "Ever stalked deer, Cord? I've tried it a few times, back home, in the Highlands."

"Meaning?"

"That it helps to be lucky. I only shot one once — an' it practically gave itself up."

"Thanks," said Cord sardonically. He braced himself into a more comfortable position, located a cheroot, and sucked it thoughtfully. Luck always played its part — but he'd been using more than his share of it lately, might fast be

213

approaching the risk of overdrawing his account. He sighed, settled back, and watched the scrubland go past through half-shut eyes.

Within an hour any suggestion of a road was far behind them and they were travelling over a barren, desert-like expanse of empty, featureless terrain. The temperature gauge on the Ford's panel climbed higher towards the red boiling-point line, sweat trickled down Spence's thin, worn face like so many rivulets, and Cord felt an oppressive, baked, lethargy seeping its way through his bones.

The way grew rougher, the springs heaved a growing protest, the dust film on the windshield gradually thickened. Twice Spence slowed his pace, as if uncertain, then made up his mind and pressed on again.

They'd covered forty-two miles by the speedometer's reading — forty-two miles in a fraction under three hours — when Cord heard the man give a sudden grunt of satisfaction.

"The map's right so far — two hills, one like a clenched fist, the other wi' a rock slide down its east face. That looks like them ahead."

In a matter of minutes they were close enough to be sure — the first stage was over. Spence steered for a patch of shadow near the foot of the rock slide and stopped. Then he gave a long groan of relief, reached behind him, brought out a canteen, and took a long drink of water before passing it over.

"Aye, and now for a hike, eh?" he said wryly.

Cord took his time about answering, seeing the man's tired eyes, the weary droop of his shoulders, the still stubborn determination which on its own wasn't enough.

"My hike, John." As Spence's mouth hardened, he went on quickly, emphatically. "Suppose we were both in there and we had to run like hell to get back out — how long would you last?"

"If you mean — "

"I mean you got me here and now you stay. You know why."

Their eyes clashed for a long moment then, reluctantly, Spence looked away. "It's a few years since I went chasing over hills," he admitted slowly. "I'll be here till you get back."

"Or till dusk."

Spence nodded.

★ ★ ★

Cord went in with a canteen of water over one shoulder, Spence's binoculars slung round his neck and a pair of native sandals on his feet. The sandals had been Spence's idea — he'd had two pairs in the brown paper parcel beneath the utility seat, and it made sense that a set of European shoetracks would be tantamount to shouting a warning if one of Darrald's game rangers came by. But Cord had turned down the offered rifle, just so much extra weight to slow him down. And he kept his own lightweight moccasins, crammed into the hip pocket of his slacks.

From the foot of the hill where the utility was parked the pencilled map guided him south through a maze of broken rock, heavily laced with scrub and alive with ants. He set himself a steady pace, using cover when it was available, avoiding the open stretches if he could, eyes constantly scanning ahead, ears strained for the slightest alien sound. Further on, where the ground began rising, the poacher's route led to a long, narrow crack in the rock, half-choked with thorns, ideal for snakes. He moved warily, the crack thinned and threatened to disappear — then suddenly it widened again and there was open ground beyond once more.

It was the boundary edge of the Sanctuary. Whatever, whoever was beyond was his enemy. He rested for a moment, used the binoculars then walked on.

Another half-mile was behind him

when he heard the approaching engine, still faint, but a hum growing by the moment. Cord dived for the nearest thicket of thornbush, threw himself flat, burrowed as far under its fishhooked branches as he could, then waited, the Neuhausen in his hand.

Painted sand grey, the jeep came into sight and headed in his direction at a slow, deliberate pace. It had a crew of two aboard. Both wore khaki shirts and bright pink berets and the man by the driver's side carried an automatic rifle across his knees. Cord hugged the ground as the vehicle came opposite, then it had passed, continuing its steady patrol.

As the sound died in the distance Cord drew a thankful breath, wriggled out of cover, and checked the map. It's next reference point, a ridge of hills, lay to the south-west another three or so miles on. He set off, trudging deeper and deeper into the Sanctuary, his thong-fastened sandals travelling for a spell over a hard, broken mosaic of sun-baked clay as he followed the course of a dried-out stream bed.

The hills grew near. He chose one higher than the rest as potential observation point, started scrambling up its steep slope, and was panting heavily long before he reached the top. When he got there he threw himself down with a grunt of relief, took a long drink from the canteen, then rested for a minute. Time was getting on — with a sigh he wiped the sweat from his forehead, dragged out the binoculars, and turned their lenses on the new valley which lay below. It was about a mile wide and fairly level. It had coarse grass and some trees — except for the central strip.

That strip — he peered down at it in incredulous disbelief then slowly lowered the binoculars and rubbed the back of his hand across aching eyes. Down there the ground was pockmarked with all too familiar craters, rutted by vehicle tracks, speckled here and there by shallow foxhole trenches. A clump of broad tall trees had been reduced to gaunt, blackened skeletons. Others were mere smashed stumps ringed by more craters.

Cord swore softly, abandoned caution, and made a fast, scrambling, downhill descent to the valley floor. As he reached the strip, he slowed, walking carefully, knowing now why wild life had long since fled the Sanctuary.

Lucas Darrald had his own private battle-training ground. Mortar bomb splinters, the glinting brass of empty cartridge cases, the sight of a straw dummy with its head blown from its shoulders, told their own story. It would have taken a flame-thrower to burn some of that tough, almost indestructible scrub to such a crisp, black powder, a heavy machine gun to have punched such a neat pattern of bullet-holes in the overturned wooden mock-up of a truck's silhouette.

The vehicle tracks led to the far end of the valley — and Cord felt very small, alone, and momentarily helpless, with the chill knowledge that already he might be framed in someone's rifle-sight.

He made back for the high ground, toiled up close to the hill's crest, then moved along, keeping parallel with the wheel ruts below. He stopped, used the binoculars again, and refocussed as he found what was now inevitable.

There was the rest of it. Hidden till then by the lie of the hills, a broad pocket of a defile led off the main valley. Like an axe wound in the living rock which formed a sheer face on three sides, it was little more than three hundred yards wide at its only entrance and perhaps four times that in length. He could count six long, camouflaged huts grouped together close under the rock at its far end, a vehicle drawn up outside one, some men moving near it.

What mattered now was to get out, get back, and let others know. Cord put the binoculars back in their case, fastened them down, and crept back over the brow of the hill.

The return journey seemed somehow easier, swifter, with familiar landmarks appearing one by one. He set himself a fast, gruelling pace, ignoring weary muscles, trying to gain and hold a constant rhythm of movement.

He grew careless.

Blundering out from a Walt Disney fantasy of high, jagged rocks he saw the jeep when it was already almost too late. Stopped about eighty yards away, the two-man crew were taking a break, squatting on the ground in the shelter of its shadow. One was smoking a cigarette . . . they were a different pair from the men he'd seen earlier, but in the same khaki uniforms and pink berets.

For a startled fraction of a second Cord stood there, paralysed. Then he slipped quickly back among the rocks, cursing his own stupidity. Moving further into cover, he squeezed past one heavy boulder, dislodged a football-sized lump of stone, and winced as it crashed down on the other boulders below.

Whatever they hadn't seen, the jeep patrolmen had now heard. Cord pulled himself higher up among the rocks before he risked looking down from cover. Both men were on their feet, rifles ready but their attitude uncertain. One pointed in Cord's general direction and they spoke briefly. A moment later the man who had pointed began walking towards the start of the rocks while his crew-mate stayed by the jeep, his rifle lowered again.

A tall, muscular figure with prominent tribal scars on both cheeks, the first patrolman grew more cautious as he widened the distance. Then he had disappeared, and Cord was left with the sound of his feet crunching over the gravelled debris, coming steadily nearer.

Gently, he slid the Neuhausen's safety catch to off, then remembered the native sandals on his feet and had a better idea. He had to move back a few yards to find what he wanted, a place where he could climb still higher yet keep below the line of vision of the man still down at the jeep.

The footsteps came closer, there was a brief glimpse of a pink beret moving between the rocks a matter of yards away. Cord took one of the spare clips of ammunition from his pocket and tossed it down to the ground. It landed with a metallic clatter, there was an immediate scuffle of feet over the loose pebbles, and the patrolman loped into view, rifle at the ready, his face eager with anticipation.

The man stopped, puzzled, then saw the clip, crossed over, and bent to lift it.

Cord jumped. His two feet landed high on the man's back, using it as a springboard. As the Moyallan cried out and went sprawling, his rifle falling with a clang, Cord was on him again. The barrel of the Neuhausen cracked against the skull beneath the beret, but its victim didn't fold, only shook his head like an angered bull and kept on rising. His eyes were on Cord, his face twisted in startling realisation that this was no easy-prey poacher, no ordinary intruder. One hand groped for the rifle as he opened his mouth to yell.

The sound didn't come. Cord reached the rifle first, seized a two-handed grip on the barrel, and swept it round in a savage arc. The butt took the man on the neck, high behind the left ear, with a bone-shattering crunch.

He was dead before he hit the ground.

Breathing heavily, his mouth suddenly dry, Cord grabbed the Neuhausen clip and put it back with the other spares. Then he bent down, snapped the thongs which held the sandle on his left foot, dropped it close by the dead man's body, and quickly removed its twin. It took only seconds to drag his own moccasins from his hip pocket, pull them on, and stow the sandal in their place.

He hadn't gone many yards when

the jeep's horn sounded anxiously from beyond the rocks. Cursing, Cord triggered two swift shots from the rifle in the general direction of the vehicle and hurried on again, travelling fast, avoiding any soft patch of sand or gravel where he might leave anything approaching a footprint. At first, he concentrated on distance only, then gradually changed his route, coming round in a wide circle which would take him clear of the place where he'd had to kill.

After fifteen minutes he was clear of the nightmare of rocks, back on rolling bushland. Panting, he dropped down in the shelter of a patch of scrub, shoved the rifle deep under the bushes, and rested briefly. Then, after another long drink of lukewarm water from the canteen, he rose to his feet and started the job of picking up the route back to where Spence would be waiting.

Behind him, he reckoned, he'd left one very worried patrolman. His comrade dead and the man's rifle missing, the remaining half of the jeep's crew would have to be a particularly determined character to start a pursuit on his own — a pursuit after a poacher who had lost a sandal in that deadly struggle but who was now armed on equal terms.

The rest of the way was clear. Twice, as he neared the Sanctuary's boundary, Cord saw vehicles in the distance, moving fast as if quartering the area. But now the advantage was his, he was on his way out, they were searching blind.

The sun was low on the western skyline when he crossed the last weary stretch of scrub towards the hill with the long gash on its side. As he drew nearer and saw the Ford at the bottom of the slope, a shrill whistle rang out and John Spence came hurrying to meet him.

Spence sized him up at a glance and led the way to the utility.

"Get in," growled the Scot. "Get some food in your belly while I drive.

I've a feeling we'd best be out o' here."

Cord grinned weakly, his face twisting along the path of the scar on his cheek.

"Do that," he agreed hastily. "I'm not arguing."

6

NIGHT had fallen long before the Ford reached El Wabir, but Talos Cord almost welcomed the bouncing monotony of the return trip. Once he'd told John Spence what had happened he sat silent and let the miles go by, his mind battling with the problems ahead, problems fast approaching boiling point.

A whole section of the puzzle now clicked into place. The cynically named Sanctuary was more than a depot for smuggled munition — it was a training ground for men to operate the weapons being purchased, men who could go on to give at least a rudimentary instruction to the rebel soldiery equipped by each deal.

Robert Tollogo had managed to insinuate himself into one of these hard-core groups which moved in and out of Moyalla under the camouflage of contract workers. But Tollogo's class had no sooner graduated than it had been wiped out in the plane crash.

To remove one man — or because only the existence of an outsider was known, not his identity? Even so, that left the death of Frank Darrald. The Sanctuary set-up might guard its business interests with ruthless care, but would it even sacrifice the *Tillik Sau*'s son in the process?

The utility lurched heavily then settled into a happier pace as its wheels met the smoother surface of a well-defined track. Cord glanced at his watch. It was nearly 9 p.m.

"David Saat should be at the police barracks," said Spence suddenly, as if reading his mind. "Want to try there first?"

Cord nodded. "We'd better. Think anyone will have been looking for us?"

"It's likely." Spence pursed his lips. "I told Sildo he was to say you'd gone out on calls again wi' me that we'd be late back. Still . . . " he shrugged. "I wouldn't count on that sandal trick o' yours doing more than winning a little time."

"If it does even that I'm happy."

"Aye." The Scot gave a faint sigh of relief as their headlamps found the first huts of the village.

El Wabir's police barracks was a big concrete shoebox of a building located conveniently near to its main source of business, the local beerhall, with a cell-block and living quarters at the rear. Spence parked to one side of the building and they went in. An askari corporal lounging in the outer office snapped upright as they entered, greeted them with a grin, and led the way down a narrow, whitewashed corridor. Saat's office was a small, square room with space for a desk and a few chairs, a large, framed portrait of Moyalla's current president occupying a prominent position on one wall.

The corporal left them, and in a few

moments Saat hurried in, his uniform jacket half-fastened, a look of relief on his broad face.

"*Vizuri* . . . it takes a weight off my mind to see you both back." His eyes and mouth creased at the thought. "It would have been difficult to decide what to do if you had, well, vanished."

He waved them into chairs, produced his cigarettes and, once they were lit, leaned back against the edge of his desk with hopeful interest. "Here, things have been busy and promising — and with you?"

"Fairly interesting." Cord took a long draw on his cigarette, let the smoke trickle towards the low ceiling, and began. By the time he'd finished, Saat's face was a study in grim dismay.

"This place — and in my district." He gave something close to a groan. "It is a job for troops, but to ask for such help would be a waste of time. The army is already stretched to the limit to cope with our political problems in the north." Another thought struck him and worsened the situation. "And whatever happens, when I make my report to Nygall there is a certain chief superintendent of police who will demand more than mere explanations."

"Man, you can't be blamed," protested Spence. "That valley is miles inside Darrald's empire. Nobody goes there, no planes fly over. How could you have known?"

"I hope others are equally under-standing," said Saat with little hope in his voice. He shook his head. "Still, that is secondary. What has been happening here matters too — and requires decisions."

Cord raised an eyebrow. "Our deputation from the Congo have arrived?"

"I think so." Saat drew a small, stiff-covered notebook from one pocket and tapped it briefly. "The details are simple enough. I had a watch on the airstrip and another on the warehouse, as arranged."

"Your men knew why?"

The Moyallan's shoulders straightened. "They are my men they obey orders. Nothing has happened at the airstrip. But at noon there was an arrival at the warehouse, a car belonging to the *Tillik Sau*. Nyeme and the man Sydney Holt from the chemical plant were aboard, with a driver. In a little under half an hour the car left again, without Nyeme but with Jean Berry in the rear seat beside the man Holt."

"Damned strange for a start," grunted Spence. "She can't stand him."

"If I can go on?" Saat cleared his throat reproachfully, flicked open the notebook, and consulted it for a moment. "Nothing more happened until a few minutes before 4 p.m. Then a truck arrived from the coast road, was let into the warehouse yard by Berry, and drove straight into the building. It left soon afterwards and returned towards the coast. I had — ah — arranged for it to be stopped in the next district on the return journey, on the excuse of the search for the man Wani. The driver's papers showed the truck was hired to carry Mid-Con drilling stores to El Wabir and of course it was empty on the return trip." He rubbed the edge of the notebook along his chin. "All I will say is that the askari I had on watch reported the vehicle sat high on its springs when it arrived here, as if it carried little cargo."

"Nothing more than a few men," said Cord. "Nicely done."

Saat smiled a little at the implied compliment. "One day, Mr Cord, I will tell you of our police training school at Nygall. It is run by an excellent principal who had to retire from the French Sûreté under unfortunate circumstances but there is a little more. At 6 p.m. a car collects Nyeme and he goes away. A little later, Hal Berry leaves and is now at home."

"And still no sign of his sister?"

"None," said Saat quietly. "But there are two other matters. First, the sergeant who went to Number

Five drilling site returned a short time ago. He found that your friend Tollogo arrived there originally, but after a few days he was transferred to Number Four site. My sergeant went there. They had no knowledge of this transfer — the man never arrived."

"Who arranged it?"

"Berry." Saat growled the name angrily. "He organises the supply of contract labour. It would seem that it is fairly simple to make a man vanish in this way and not be missed — one man or several."

Spence shifted awkwardly in his chair, finding it hard to follow. "You mean Berry can bring them in, pretend to transfer them and — "

"And move them into the Sanctuary instead," completed Cord stonily. "The sites don't spot what's going on and he stays in the clear. But tomorrow's load is different. He'll have to take them straight to the Sanctuary."

Saat put the notebook away and nodded. "In case he decides to leave — ah — unexpectedly, there is still a watch on the warehouse. But like you, I would like to know where his sister has gone and why."

"It worries me." John Spence scowled across the room. "All right, Cord says she tried to lure him off this morning. Maybe it looks as though she's hiding something." His face reddened a little. "I just happen to like the girl — and how do we know what's happening?"

"We must wait and see," admitted Saat soothingly. "I have a wife who would be hard to convince if the young lady ended up in one of my cells." He glanced towards Cord. "The other matter is one I intend to check on now. It may mean nothing, but — well, it is worth the journey."

"Where?"

"The chemical plant. The corporal outside has a friend who is a labourer at the digging area, a distant cousin of some sort. The man arrived in the village this evening and after he had been in the beerhall for a little it was necessary to arrest him." Saat's face stayed impassive but there was a slight twinkle in his eyes. "There will be no charge, but we will hold on to him for the moment — and I have talked to the man. There is a new trench at the soda lake, one not long started. Yesterday morning, it seems, part of it was found collapsed. The workers were told the rest should be filled in, that the Bwana Holt did not want to risk an accident."

Cord whistled softly, looked around for an ashtray, saw there was none, and stubbed his cigarette on the floor. "Wani?"

"I would like to find out, Mr Cord."

"Wait now," said Spence cautiously. "That means driving past Darrald's place."

"Not the way I will go," said Saat confidently. "This — "

"Is your district," Cord finished for him with a faint smile on his lips. "Want either of us along?"

The policeman shook his head. "I

have two of my men and the corporal's cousin waiting outside. But if one of you could stay here till I return then it would help."

They nodded agreement, and Saat was happy. He stood up, fastened the rest of his tunic, and moved towards the door.

"David, about Jean Berry," persisted Spence. "You'll not do anything — well, hasty?"

"I do not want to," qualified Saat. He glanced briefly at Cord, shrugged, and went out. As his footsteps died away along the corridor Cord yawned, moved his chair, and swung his feet up to rest on the policeman's desk. Then he glanced at Spence and his eyes narrowed a little.

The F.A.O. man was sitting quietly, his weariness plain, his thin face pale beneath that surface tan. Two long, punishing spells behind the utility's wheel had taken their toll. Cord left him a few moments more then spoke.

"John — "

"Uh?" A tired gaze met his own.

"We don't both need to stay." He tried to handle it diplomatically. "One of us would do — and I've a signal I want radioed to Nygall."

"Then go and send it," said Spence, pulling himself into a more upright position. "Unless you want rid o' me."

"That's not what I mean," Cord sighed and shook his head. "You know it too, so where's the sense in it?"

Spence sucked his teeth, looked away, then gave in. "Like I said before, I'm all right, what's the message?"

Cord borrowed a pencil and paper from Saat's desk, wrote slowly and carefully, then handed it over.

"Code?" Spence raised an eyebrow as he glanced at the sheet.

"A few things I think we're going to need," said Cord. "Duvert is flying in vaccine for you tomorrow, isn't he?" As Spence nodded, he went on, "Then this will be the rest of the load. I radioed this morning saying I might need some stuff in a hurry."

"Will there be a reply?"

"Probably, a plain-language confirmation. I don't need to know about it. And if anything happens here I'll get word to you straight away."

"Aye." Spence folded the paper, put it in his pocket, and rose. "Just make sure you don't forget."

Once he'd gone, Cord gave a wry chuckle, fished out a cheroot, lit it, and stared lazily at the portrait on the wall. Moyalla's premier had been pictured with what was probably meant to be an anti-imperialistic outthrust of his chin. The politician had been in office for four months, a reasonable record by local standards. With luck and the army behind him he might last longer than some of his predecessors — and as long as the situation remained as it was, reasonably legal and reasonably peaceful, Field Reconnaissance weren't concerned.

The cheroot was down to its final inch when there was a brief tap on the door and the askari corporal looked in.

"*Bwana* — "

He swung his feet down almost guiltily from the desk under the man's slightly reproachful gaze. "Yes?"

"It is the *Tillik Sau*'s daughter, Missie Paula — "

"What about her?" Cord's laziness evaporated at the words.

The corporal hesitated. "All I know, *bwana*, is that she has arrived along at the Bwana Berry's house. The message has just come."

Cord rose to his feet, frowning. "*Ahasante*," he thanked the man. "If there is more I want to hear."

The corporal nodded, went out, but seemed gone only a matter of minutes before he was back, this time openly perturbed, glancing warily over his shoulder.

"*Bwana*, she is here — "

"And I haven't much time." A slim, impatient figure in a tightly belted white dustcoat brushed past him into the room. "Talos, it's important." Paula Darrald's face was pale and he saw the way her hands clenched nervously at her sides.

He nodded to the corporal, who left thankfully. "What's wrong, Paula?"

She moved perhaps six inches, her eyes never leaving his face. Part of his mind registered that under the dustcoat she was wearing a dress he hadn't seen before, high-collared, in a pale cornflower blue.

"I came to see David Saat," she said quickly. "But I hoped you'd be here too."

"He had to go out on an inquiry. Still if I can help — "

"You can." The desperate note in her voice silenced him. "Let's stop pretending, Talos. Either — either agree that you understand what I'm talking about, or that you know enough to be able to tell someone who will. Richard and my father are holding Jean out at the Sanctuary so they can be sure Hal Berry will go through with tomorrow's delivery." She took a deep breath, as if the worst was over.

"They've got one opinion about you — I've got another. So I made the excuse of coming in to tell Hal again that she'd be all right as long as he did what they wanted. And — well, here I am."

Cord took her firmly by the shoulders and made her sit in the nearest chair. He stood looking at her, his face serious, trying to make up his mind just how far he could trust this girl.

His silence was eloquent enough for Paula to understand.

"I'm here for two reasons," she said slowly and deliberately. "The first is that I don't think they can let Jean or Hal go after this. The second . . . " she bit hard on her lip then looked away. "The second is because I think my father let Frank die in that plane though he could have stopped it happening. I've had enough, more than enough."

He made his decision.

"Paula . . . " he waited until her eyes met his own. "How long have you known what goes on in the Sanctuary?"

"Long enough," she admitted, her voice suddenly flat and colourless. "The gun-running began about three years ago. My father and Richard started it between them, and when I found out — " she shrugged unhappily. "Well, I'm away most of the time. Even if I'd wanted, what could I have done? Then it began to grow, get — bigger and bigger . . . " she looked at him for some encouragement, seemed to find it, and went on. "Talos, I didn't know how big, not till I came out after Frank died. I — I didn't know they were prepared to murder if it was necessary."

"What about Frank? Was he in the partnership?"

"He knew about it. But he wanted to be a lumber man." A wealth of unsaid information lay behind the words.

"And you say your father let him die — "

"I think . . . yes, I know he did. Because there was someone else on that plane they wanted to kill."

"A friend of mine," said Cord

quietly. "What makes you so sure about it, Paula?"

She fumbled in one pocket of her coat, pulled out her cigarette case, and lit one with hands that trembled just a little.

"Something Hal Berry told Jean last night. I didn't know about it until she was brought out this afternoon and — well, we had a chance to talk. I hadn't been told they were going to more or less use her as a hostage — not till then. Jean said she'd been sent to try and draw you away this morning and when it didn't work Hal had — well, he thought they'd just have to kill you." She swallowed. "He said that if a man could sabotage a plane and let his own son be killed in the process he was ruthless enough for anything."

"You knew what was going to happen when you took me to the lumber camp?"

She flushed and drew quickly on the cigarette. "Only partly, believe me. Richard promised they were only going to scare you — that having you around was becoming awkward. He said you were just a minor form-filling nuisance."

Cord raised a sardonic eyebrow. "You decided differently?"

Something which at another time might have been the beginning of a smile touched her mouth. "I was there — he wasn't."

He nodded slowly. "All right, Paula. And when you came here, what did you want me to do?"

"Stop it, stop it before more people get killed, people like Jean."

"You know what that could mean as far as your father is concerned?"

She got up, the glare of the overhead light making her hair glint like spun gold. Her mouth tightened and she nodded.

"I'll go now," she said quietly. "They'd ask questions if I stayed away too long. Just one other thing, Talos. Someone killed a patrolman in the Sanctuary today. They think it was probably some stray *shifta* bandit — but they're getting nervous. I — I'd be very careful."

Cord started to speak then decided against it. Silently, he stood aside to let her pass. He stood where he was, giving her ample time to leave the barracks and be well clear, then strode through to the outer office.

"*Bwana?*" The corporal laid down a comic book he'd been reading and glanced significantly towards the outer doorway.

"I'm going to the Mid-Con office," Cord told him. "While I'm there I don't want to be disturbed. Can you get that message to the man on watch? *Umeelewa?*"

"*Ndio, bwana,*" said the corporal, a gleam entering his eyes. "I understand. You will not be — too noisy, *bwana?*"

"I will not be too noisy," Cord assured him.

The corporal looked again at that hard, scarred face and decided that perhaps after all there were worse things in life than wearing a blue uniform and holding the keys to El Wabir's cells.

* ★ *

Except for a light at one window on the upper floor, the Mid-Con building was in darkness. Cord stared up at it for a moment then tried the front door, found it locked, and hammered his fist on the wooden panels. There was no answer. He tried again, swore under his breath as still nothing happened, and walked quietly down the alleyway to the rear of the two-storey structure. Another, smaller door was there, half-hidden in the shadows.

Cord tried the handle then took a half-step back and swung his foot. The heel of his shoe hit the wood with near scientific accuracy exactly two inches below the lock, the ideal pressure point, and the door burst open with little more noise than an air-filled paper bag. He went in quickly, closed the door behind him again, and listened. Somewhere above his head a floorboard creaked and a voice muttered a nervous curse.

Softly, carefully, Cord took a few steps forward. A door creaked open, light spilled out from the room above, and he had his bearings. He was in a small hallway beside the stairs leading to the Berry living quarters.

"Take it easy, Hal," he advised loudly. "It's Cord — I'm alone."

A cautious figure moved a little way down the stairway, peering into the darkness. Hal Berry had a revolver in one hand, pointing it uncertainly in his general direction.

"I'll come up," said Cord, in the same loud, confident voice. "I tried the front door, but nobody answered. There was that light burning, so I thought I'd better get in fast in case something was wrong." As he spoke, he had reached the stairs and was approaching the man, moving briskly and with an air of cheerful apology.

"Everything's all right?"

"Fine." Berry still held the gun uncertainly. His pudgy face was unshaven, the hair tousled, he wore a crumpled, stained workshirt and denims. The blue eyes flickered nervously. "Look, what the hell — "

"Let's point this somewhere else." Cord reached out, gripped the revolver by its barrel, and took it from the man's unprotesting fingers. "Now then . . . " he led the way into the room, and stood waiting till Berry had followed him in. A bottle and a half-filled glass stood on the floor beside one of the chairs. He crossed over, picked up the glass, and sniffed. "Having a little party to yourself, Hal?"

Berry's mouth twisted in an angry protest. "I asked — " he stopped short as he saw the ice-cold expression on his visitor's face.

"I'll ask," said Cord softly. He looked at the gun in his hand, laid it down on a table, and turned back to the Mid-Con man. "Feeling frightened,

Hal — frightened about what's going to happen to your sister if you don't go through with tomorrow? Or — " he cocked his head a little to one side " — maybe you're more frightened on your own behalf. Which is it?"

Berry stared at him, breathing through his mouth, his eyes suddenly sick with fear. "I don't want you here — go on, get back out."

"Different from the gold-smuggling business, isn't it," mused Cord, his voice stabbing like a sharp needle. "She's out at the Sanctuary right now. And you've every right to be frightened, Hal. One way or another it looks like you're both scheduled for the killing bottle before this is over. Darrald and Nyeme don't believe in leaving things to chance. After tomorrow's over you'll both know too much." Deliberately, gambling, he turned his back. "But they'll do it neatly. Maybe the land-train will be found somewhere between here and the drilling site. You and your sister aboard, dead — some wandering bunch of those *shifta* bandits you're so keen to warn people — "

He sensed as much as heard the man draw a sudden breath and dive towards the table. Berry's fingers were still clawing towards the gun when he swung round, his left fist slamming like a piston into the barrel-chested man's middle, his right sending the weapon flying far into one corner of the room.

With an explosive wheeze of pain, Berry practically hinged at the waist then made a desperate attempt to keep coming on. Cord took a half-step to the right, let the man begin to straighten, then hit him again in exactly the same spot. Once more Berry began to fold — but Cord seized him by the shirt, jerked him upright, and brushed aside a weak, wildly aimed blow. The man stood there, swaying, and Cord almost sighed as he drove a third, pounding left into that battered middle. It was time to finish it. The edge of his hand chopped down and took Berry just behind and below the ear.

The Mid-Con man's eyes glazed, he tried to stay upright, then pitched forward on his face.

Cord looked down at him for a moment, before he went through to the kitchen of the flat, switched on the light, and ran cold water into the sink until it was full almost to the brim. He went back, gripped Berry under the arms, dragged him through, propped him up against the sink, and pushed his head into the water.

Pulled out at the count of five, Berry came up spluttering feebly. As he gasped air, Cord rammed his head down into the water again, counted, and jerked him up by the hair.

"Don't — " the nasal whine died in a frantic gurgle as the terrified, unshaven face submerged for the third time. When Cord pulled the man up the abject fear quivering on his features was enough. Cord let go, and the bulky figure clung to the sink for support, shaking.

Something close to pity entered Cord's mind, but there was too much at stake. He bent down, turned Berry's face roughly to the light and let him see the cold purpose he'd unleashed.

"You've got the Congo buying party in the warehouse. How many of them?"

"Four . . . " Berry groaned and tried to look away.

"Who else is there?"

"My — my nightguard." Berry shuddered violently and seemed ready to be sick.

"That's all?"

The nod wasn't enough. Cord started to push him back towards the water.

"One — one of Nyeme's men came with them. That's all, it's the truth."

Cord relaxed his grip. "Now the rest of it. What's the delivery arrangement?"

Berry nodded and licked his lips. "By the land-train — just the tractor. I've got to take them straight to the Sanctuary."

"Fine," Cord congratulated him with an icy grin. "You're scared, Berry — with reason. African jails rate pretty low on any list, but they're not as permanent as a bullet. And there getting too risky. So — " he swallowed " — they said they'd take her?"

The man winced. "I didn't want to make this — this run. I'd taken enough risks for them, I'd a hunch things were getting too risky. So — " he swallowed " — they said they'd have to make sure I didn't do anything foolish."

"And left you sweating." At least he'd stayed, hadn't run out on his own — it was always something. "How much did Jean know about what was going on?"

"Nothing . . . " Berry avoided his gaze . . . "not till last night, when they started putting the pressure on. She . . . " he licked his lips again " . . . she started worrying once or twice when she saw I'd some extra cash, but I spun her a story about the poker games out at the drilling sites." He started to struggle to his feet.

"Not yet." Cord shoved him down

again. "How'd you get into this, Berry? Did Darrald find out you were working a fast one on Mid-Con over those paysheets — drawing money for campboys who didn't exist, was that it?"

"Does it matter?" The man gathered scanty courage for a brief moment. "I want — " he stopped short as Cord suddenly gripped him by the hair again. "Yes . . ."

"And it gave him the idea of bringing in men by using the Mid-Con route?"

Berry tried to nod, then, his eyes widening, he stared over Cord's shoulder towards the doorway. A faint chuckle from behind made Cord freeze then release his grip and turn slowly.

"Would this be what — ah — is known as psychological methods, Mr Cord?" queried David Saat. The Moyallan came into the room, his broad lips parted in a mild, inquiring smile, his shoes and trouser legs stained with the grey mud of the soda lake, the fly-whisk in his hand swinging lightly. He crossed to the sink, raised an eyebrow, and glanced at Cord. "I know there is a European saying about washing dirty linen, but this is the first time I have seen it practised."

The smile faded. "Perhaps it would have been easier to persuade your friend if he had been with me, if he had seen what I have seen."

"You found Wani?" asked Cord, already certain of the answer.

"Where we expected." Saat's voice became grim. "The hyenas were already trying to dig down to him, which made the job that little easier." The Moyallan shrugged. "He had been shot through the back of the head. We left him there for obvious reasons."

Hal Berry stared at Saat in a mixture of horror and disbelief. But it was Cord who answered the question on his lips.

"Balder and Wani — two more for Darrald's list, Berry."

"But — but why?"

"Maybe that's for you to answer,"

rapped Cord. He saw Saat's fly-whisk stop in midswing as he went on. "You're the man who said that Darrald was ruthless enough to let his son be killed in that plane."

Berry scrambled to his feet, and this time Cord didn't try to stop him. "The only person I told about that — "

"Was your sister," nodded Cord.

"Perhaps Mr Berry could use a cigarette," murmured Saat. He produced his own, gave one to the man, and lit it with a match. "Now, Mr Berry, I am another who thinks you should tell us a little more."

The Mid-Con man drew hard on the cigarette, a broken shadow of his one-time pugnaciously confident self. "I — I was at the airstrip that day."

"You brought in the batch of men who'd finished training at the Sanctuary?" nodded Cord. "Then what?"

"I loaded them aboard the transport plane and went over to the hut to have a beer with Balder." Berry gnawed his lip. "Look, they let Frank go on that plane, didn't try to stop him. Frank was flying to the coast in the *Tillik Sau*'s own plane with Nyeme piloting. But — well, something went wrong — something mechanical, right on take-off. Balder even had the flight in his log book and had to cancel the entry." He missed the flicker of understanding that passed between his two inquisitors. "Next thing I saw from the hut was Nyeme walking Frank over to the transport. The devil was cold-blooded enough to stand out there and wave goodbye as it took off. Then — " he shrugged his misery. "Well, it crashed. And Nyeme just walked over to the hut, told us we'd never seen him, went out to the car he had waiting, and drove away. Didn't stay, just — just drove away."

"Mr Berry." David Saat's voice was chill and precise. "Did you know that plane was going to crash?"

"No." Berry shook his head in anxious haste. "But Nyeme — well, he'd told me before I collected the squad from the Sanctuary that I was to make sure nobody tried to get away from the rest. He said there was something wrong, something they were going to take care of before the squad got clear of Lake Calu."

"Did you ever ask him what he'd meant?"

Berry shook his head but said nothing.

"Pah. No doubt you felt that would require a certain bravery," suggested Saat contemptuously. "More than was needed to arrange the ambush last night for Mr Cord."

"They were only told to rough him up," muttered Berry sullenly, looking as if he was close to crying.

"The rest can wait," said Cord, glancing at his watch. "Maybe it's time we paid a call at the warehouse before the new arrivals get restless."

"An excellent idea," murmured David Saat. "I have two men outside. One can stay to make sure your friend does nothing foolish, the other is my servant, who would be annoyed if he was left out of things."

"Then we'll take the keys." Cord held out his hand. "Berry — "

The Mid-Con man's mouth twisted bitterly as he fumbled in a pocket and handed over his key-ring.

"And where do we look for your visitors?" queried Saat in a mildly sardonic voice, the fly-whisk swinging casually.

Berry shrugged, beyond caring about anything except his immediate future. "In a cellar near the back they're down there till morning."

"Not now," corrected Saat cheerfully. "It is only hospitable to offer them — ah — alternative accommodation. I have the cells to spare."

* * *

The Mid-Con warehouse was in darkness, the land-train still parked as before in the yard outside, the wire strands of the high fence glinting here and there in the moonlight. Saat glanced around, loosened the Webley pistol at his belt, then nodded to his sergeant — a glum, silent man who carried a Patchet gun with hopeful care.

The sergeant slipped away and returned a moment later with another figure by his side, the askari constable who'd been assigned to watch the building. Saat spoke to him briefly then turned to Cord.

"They are still there," he said softly. "You have the keys — " one hand waved an invitation.

The largest of Berry's keys opened the gate in the fence. They moved stealthily into the yard, crossed to the warehouse door, and hugged the wall while Cord repeated the process. The lock clicked, the door swung open, and they tip-toed in. Lights glowed down on the silent aisles of packing cases and stores. The constable cleared his throat, a low nervous sound, drew a glare from Saat, blinked apologetically and gripped his rifle more firmly.

A silent wave of Saat's hand and they fanned out a little, easing forward, freezing as a door slammed somewhere ahead. Next moment voices sounded, footsteps rang loudly on the concrete floor, and Cord tensed.

A split second later two men turned into the main storage aisle some thirty feet away. One was Berry's night guard, an automatic jammed in the waistband of his slacks. The other, a stranger in denim overalls, nursed a sawn-off shotgun in the crook of one arm. Their mouths fell open as they saw the waiting quartet, then, without a word, they reacted. Berry's guard dived for cover, clawing for his weapon. The stranger swung his shotgun in a blurring arc — and the warehouse echoed to the rasping, coughing blast as the askari sergeant's Patchet gun cut loose.

A full half-magazine hosepiped down the aisle, smashed into the man, seemed to pick him up, then tossed him to the floor, the shotgun still unfired.

"*Endelea* . . . move!" Saat urged them forward then swore angrily as two shots cracked out from behind a high packing case and whipped the air near his head. There was a fresh patter of running feet as the night guard sprinted further back into the warehouse. Another shot, and the sergeant stopped, an expression of something close to indignation on his face, as he clasped one hand to the patch of blood welling high on one shoulder.

Cord saw a movement ahead, took a quick snapshot with the Neuhausen, heard a cry of pain, then hugged cover as the gun ahead fired wildly in reply. To his right, the askari constable dropped behind a mound of vehicle spares and began a systematic, pumping rifle-fire towards the spot.

"Talos . . . " Saat's loud whisper brought his head round. The policeman waved his arms in an encircling motion, Cord nodded, and they began working outward in opposite arcs. Suddenly, a figure sprang across the aisle ahead, Saat's heavy Webley barked twice, and the night guard was rolling on the floor, both hands clutching high on his left leg.

Only the wounded man's low moaning broke the silence as they walked forward. His gun was lying on the floor, and Cord kicked it clear while Saat looked down, shaking his head. Cord's bullet had grazed the — night guard's side, but the two from the Webley had taken him in mid-thigh.

"*Mtundu* . . . you foolish one," mused the Moyallan. "It will be a long time before you walk again, even with luck." He glanced round as his two men approached. "Is the other one dead — "

The sergeant nodded, holding a handkerchief to this shoulder, the blood still seeping between his fingers.

Cord left them, prowled the nearby aisles, then softly called them over and pointed to a metal hatchway set flush with the concrete.

"Ah." Saat grinned, took the sergeant's Patchet gun, and signalled to his constable. The man gripped the hatch's centre ring, heaved, and as the cover swung up Saat stuck the Patchet's muzzle into the widening gap. At last he leaned forward a little more, looked over the edge . . . and chuckled.

Down below, at the foot of a short flight of steps, four frightened black faces stared up from a small, brightly lit basement crudely furnished with four camp beds and little else. The Patchet gun beckoned, and the quartet of arms buyers practically fell over each other in their eagerness to obey and mount the stairway. As each reached the top, he clasped his hands on his head without waiting for the order.

Once they stood in line, Saat inspected them with studied care and frowned in disappointment.

"They look most ordinary. You — " he pointed to the nearest, a fat middle-aged man with a neatly trimmed goatee beard, dressed like the others in a crumpled but expensive lounge suit. "Are you ordinary?"

The fat man nodded in anxious agreement.

Saat shook his head with a sigh. "What else is down there? Talos, if you would like . . . "

Cord nodded and entered the cellar. Two large, brand new suitcases lay beside one of the camp beds, their lids double-locked.

"Perhaps these?" Saat tossed down a bundle of keys. "They were in the fat one's pocket."

The keys fitted. He snapped open the first case and whistled through his teeth. Row upon row of neat, rubber-banded bundles of banknotes filled it to the brim in a variety of currencies — American dollars, Swiss francs, British sterling and plenty more.

Saat clattered down the stairway as he opened the second suitcase and stood as if mesmerised at the sight of its identical contents.

"Have you seen so much money in one place before, Talos?"

Cord shook his head. "Not outside a bank." Maybe it was the answer. Plenty of banks had been systematically emptied in the last of the Congo's simba flare-ups. That kind of money would be almost impossible to trace back to its original source.

Wistfully, Saat closed the suitcases again, heft them by the handles with a wry respect, and followed Cord back up into the warehouse. The four Congolese were still standing in line, hands on their heads, the askari sergeant eyeing them in a way which showed nothing would suit him more than for one to make a break and give him the chance to do something about it.

"These four are my first problem," mused Saat, frowning thoughtfully. "First I must think of a charge."

"You might get them on illegal entry," nodded Cord. "But I wouldn't hope for much more."

"At least we can make sure they are

out of the way," decided Saat crisply. "Next, my sergeant and Berry's man need treatment — John Spence is good at such things, enough at least until I can have them flown out to Nygall." He scratched his chin, troubled. "But tomorrow — what happens when Darrald finds his visitors have failed to arrive?"

"I've been thinking about that." Cord looked again at the four arms buyers and reluctantly made up his mind. "The land-train is outside, we've got Berry — why disappoint Darrald?"

Saat took a moment or two to understand, then his face split in a broad grin. "You think you can — ah — persuade Berry?"

"To drive?" Cord grimaced. "I'm not saying he'll like the idea but — yes, I think so."

"Good," murmured the Moyallan happily. "In that case, I will tell you a little story, a worthwhile one."

"I remember a farmer who denied stealing another man's cow — then a third man appeared, also claiming the cow as his own. Yet the first farmer finally proved it had been his cow all along. There was a fourth man, Talos. He took the cow from the farmer's field one morning, sold it in one village, stole it back an hour later, sold it in the next village, stole it back a second time — and had returned it to the real owner's herd before it was ever missed. Two lots of money for an animal he only borrowed."

Cord smiled at the bush-country tale. "The unexpected usually pays off, I suppose."

"That is what I think," said Saat, a quiet certainty in his voice. "You are worried, Talos — it is not in your face, but behind your eyes. I think what worries you is the thought that perhaps still more men will die — black and white." He shrugged. "You talked once of walking on eggs. Surely, when that happens, a few are always broken. But I will look forward to the morning. It is not many men who have the chance to fight against an infection called war."

"Then it's settled," said Cord heavily.

It meant a gamble, and he was neither sure nor confident of the outcome. But they had surprise on their side — surprise and, if Andrew Beck had arranged things right, something more.

7

THE sun was still struggling over the horizon when the blue Marchetti droned over El Wabir airstrip, lowered its tricycle undercarriage, and touched down on the wire mesh surface in a billowing wake of dust.

Duvert was alone at the controls. He taxied the little plane round, brought it to a stop beside the airstrip hut, and was wriggling out of the cockpit canopy while the propeller was still sighing to a halt. The young, round-faced Frenchman dropped to the ground with a supple ease and inspected his welcoming committee with a frank, expectant curiosity. A huddle of waiting askaris, that great giant of a six-wheeled tractor in the background — they had told him at Nygall this would be no

273

ordinary trip and for once they'd been right.

"Good morning." His eyes twinkled at the approaching trio. "It seem's I am not the only one who had an early start to his day."

Talos Cord returned the pilot's grin and beckoned Spence and Saat nearer. "You brought everything, Duvert?"

"Everything you ordered. And to be frank, my nose troubles me with curiosity."

"You're not alone," grumbled Spence, stretching on tip-toe to peer past him into the Marchetti's cabin. "Just what is in there anyway?"

Cord grinned. "Mind if I show them, Duvert?"

"Be my guest," agreed the Frenchman cheerfully. "For the last three hours they have been terrifying me. *Ne pas toucher* . . . do not touch, that was my motto."

"They were safe enough." Cord swung himself up on the Marchetti's wing and was satisfied as he saw the neatly packed boxes which seemed to fill every spare inch of passenger space. He heaved out the nearest, handed it carefully down to Spence, and kept the rest coming in the same way until they were slid out in a long line on the runway mesh.

"You expect to win with — with just these?" David Saat's voice was faintly incredulous as he opened the lid of one box and saw the small, sausage-shaped cylinders which lay within, cylinders with two white lines painted round their middles. "Unless . . . " his eyes showed suspicion.

"Just a rather special brand of combination tear gas and chemical smoke cartridges," declared Cord reassuringly, dropping down from the plane and crossing to join him. "The British developed them, we simply made them more highly concentrated — and changed the smoke from red to dark purple. A tame psychologist in California worked out it's the colour that sends most people into a panic."

"I see. Provided, of course, they are not colour-blind." The Moyallan showed little confidence in the idea. He thumbed to a group of larger cases. "And these?"

"Three cartridge projectors, spring-powered, up to three hundred and fifty yards range. One box of smoke-masks, two walkie-talkie radios — " he glanced up at Duvert.

"And the rest as you asked," nodded the pilot. "The loud-hailer is already in position."

"Good," agreed Cord, turning back to the others. "That's the lot — except for a couple of king-sized versions of these cartridges which stay with the plane."

John Spence frowned and shook his head. "Man, I hope you know what you're doing," he said gloomily. "I'm no expert in this, but it's no' what I expected. You know what we're up against."

Cord nodded. The few hours that had passed since the warehouse raid had been busy, sobering ones with little chance for sleep. The four Congolese were refusing to do more than admit their names. He glanced over towards the waiting tractor unit and saw Hal Berry standing unhappily by the cab, an askari guard by his side. It had taken a long session, a mixture of threats and persuasion, before the Mid-Con man had reluctantly agreed to play his part. But he'd also added a little more to what they knew — between men under training, instructors and Darrald's regular guard patrols there was a force of at least forty to be dealt with in the Sanctuary.

Against that, Saat could muster less than a dozen askaris, even including the handful he'd managed to borrow from the next district. More were on their way, but it would take time for them to arrive. Too much time — when Lucas Darrald must already be preparing for the arrival of the buying delegation.

"We are not going to fight children,"

said Saat uneasily, glancing back at his men. "I had hoped for — well, something better than this."

"You praised the unexpected," reminded Cord. He tapped the nearest box with one foot. "This is it. If it works, we can do the job before they know what happened — with minimum bloodshed."

But with plenty of risk, he thought grimly.

David Saat rose to his feet with a sigh. "For all our sakes, I hope you are right. What else is to be done?"

"We need a man to fly with Duvert — someone with authority in his voice."

"That can be done," agreed Sat, smiling a little at the idea. He called over his shoulder. "*Sarjeni* . . . "

The askari sergeant, his wounded arm in a broad sling, hurried over with a hopeful look on his face.

"*Sarjeni*, you will go with the Bwana Duvert in his *ndeie*, on an important task." As the man nodded vigorously, Saat muttered to Cord, "Which disposes of a problem — that one was becoming insubordinate at the thought of being left behind."

"And me, m'sieu?" queried Duvert. "I have a rough idea what you will want done, but the details . . ."

"You'll get them," promised Cord. "Ever flown over the Sanctuary?"

"Never, I am sorry. There were complaints that such flying would frighten the wild life, and it was banned."

"It's not banned today," said Cord softly, taking a cheroot from his pocket, grimacing at its battered condition, and putting the best portion between his lips. "And I'm hoping you're going to help scare the hell out of the wild life I have in mind."

Hands in his pockets, John Spence had been listening with a slowly gathering scowl of protest. "What about me?" he demanded. "Dammit, Cord, if you're planning to squeeze me out o' this ploy too . . ."

"You've got a job all right," Cord assured him. "You'll have two of the askaris and a walkie-talkie. The moment we signal the Sanctuary's cleared you move in on Darrald's house . . ."

"Eh?" The F.A.O. man frowned. "I'd have thought you'd need every available man at the Sanctuary end."

"John, my friend, how many do you think you can cram into that tractor cabin?" asked Saat. He looked along the runway to where the sun was now a bright orange globe already warming the morning air as it climbed into the cloudless sky. "What you have to do is necessary — and perhaps difficult."

Cord nodded in tight-lipped agreement. "I want Darrald's business records before anyone tries to destroy them. If we can trace back his suppliers and where he's delivered shipments then we'll be able to stop a lot of trouble and misery in a lot of places."

"Aye." Spence showed his understanding, but rubbed one foot along the dusty ground. "And what about the girls?"

"Paula should be at the house — she's on our side, but how far she'll go along with it I don't know." More on his mind was the problem of Jean Berry, under guard at the Sanctuary, already in danger. She was another reason why surprise had to be their main hope. "Berry's sister will be our worry. Just remember, John, you don't move in at your end until we signal. The sets haven't the range to link direct, but we'll use the plane as our relay station."

Spence grunted. "I'll wait. Eh . . . if folks try to stop us?"

"You don't let them," said Cord quite simply.

★ ★ ★

The twelve massive cylinders of the giant diesel thundered to life just under half an hour later. Hal Berry, his face pale, hands tight on the steering wheel, set the tractor's big balloon tyres rolling while exhaust pulsed rhythmically from the twin stacks. It swayed gently as if happy to be released from the leash of its usual trailers, and at twenty miles an hour, sucking up a quart of diesel fuel every mile, headed towards the west, the sun at its tail, the Sanctuary on ahead.

Berry sat alone on the wide bench seat, one elbow propped on the sill of the opened window. Down beside his feet, squatting below the window level, Cord and David Saat knew they were in for an uncomfortable ride — but even so they were travelling in comparative luxury. Behind the cab, in the cramped area of the living cabin, nine askaris were packed shoulder to shoulder with their weapons and the newly arrived equipment. The door between cab and cabin had been left open to give some air circulation, but the temperature was already climbing.

"All right back there?" asked Cord.

A row of mute black faces held their own answer.

Squirming into an easier position on the metal floor, David Saat chuckled. "Sometimes the privileges of rank are welcome," he murmured, then nudged Berry. "You are sure of all that you have to do?"

"Put my neck on a chopping block — that's what it comes down to," declared Berry bitterly. He made a clumsy, grating job of changing gear, the tractor jerked, and he scowled down at them. "I'm no volunteer on this outing."

"We've no illusions, so don't worry," Cord assured him with a dry smile.

"And I've no guarantees," reminded the nasal voice in the same unhappy tone. "None for me, none for Jean — "

"No guarantees but little choice," Saat cut him short, his patience strained "You would find it difficult to help your sister from inside a cell."

"I know." The Mid-Con man turned

away from them, his mouth clamped shut, his eyes fixed on the way ahead.

Settling back, Cord tried to occupy himself by counting the rivet heads on the bumping metal floor. There was no need to ask if Berry knew the route . . . from El Wabir they were heading out on the usual Mid-Con course towards the drilling sites. But only for a few miles. Then, as Darrald had instructed him, as he'd done many times before, Berry would swing off on a cross-country leg which would take the tractor to a point where it would join the only vehicle route into the Sanctuary.

He abandoned the rivet heads and inspected the broken-nosed driver with thoughtful care. There were plenty like Hal Berry in the world, little men in eager search for easy money — just as there were always others like Lucas Darrald and Nyeme, ready to trap these little men, use them and finally dispose of them when they became an embarrassment.

Throughout their questioning Berry had denied ferrying munitions of any kind for Darrald. Cord didn't particularly believe him, didn't particularly care. The men he'd carried, raw and untrained on arrival, crash-course professionals when they left, were as dangerous as any shipment of high explosive.

For the rest? If Berry was to be believed, Lucas Darrald used his own trucks to move the tons of war material involved. The regular traffic from the chemical plant and the timber area to the coast and back was well enough established for any number of extra vehicles to operate without arousing interest. Landed at a small deep-water port on the southern coastline, moved to the supply dump in the Sanctuary, sent on from there to their final destinations, the shipments were backed by an organisation which could laugh at frontiers.

Aircraft and heavy equipment . . . well, there were ways there too when a man had contacts.

He looked in at the askaris, sweating, silent, probably apprehensive about what waited them. That was maybe how Robert Tollogo had felt three months back. And now it was time to finish what Tollogo had started. Finish it or end up dead.

It took an hour and a half of grinding, pitching travel, while the tractor's cab grew steadily warmer and the stink of diesel fumes more pronounced before, at last, they reached the top of the long slope that Cord remembered and saw the barren hills of the Sanctuary on ahead.

"Nearly there," said Berry miserably, easing his foot on the accelerator and slowing their pace to a crawl. "Better warn your friends in back, Cord."

"Just remember not to warn yours on ahead," said Cord softly. As David Saat wriggled past and squeezed into the little cabin at the rear, he eased himself up and prepared to follow. "You're on your own for the next stage, Berry. But we'll be less than a foot away. If there's trouble, you're right in the middle."

The man swallowed, nodded, and let the tractor quicken its downhill pace. Cord pushed his way into the overcrowded compartment, slid the partition door until it was only an inch or so open, and heard the askaris muttering briefly then fall suddenly silent. David Saat was at his shoulder, breathing softly, his broad face an impassive mask.

Up front, Berry changed gear again and leaned back in his seat. "Another hundred yards," he said hoarsely. "There's two of them waiting — they've a telephone line from their post to the huts, and they always check."

"Right." Cord could see for himself. A barrier pole was lowered across the track, where a small grass-thatched hut sat beside a large, painted sign which proclaimed in English and Swahili "Nature Reserve — No Entry. All Vehicles Stop' Two of Darrald's men in their khaki uniforms and pink berets stood in front of it, rifles slung over their shoulders.

He eased the Neuhausen from his pocket, slid the partition door until it was almost completely closed, and reminded Berry once again, "If they want to take a look back here it's up to you to talk them out of it."

The man gave a faint nod, and a moment later the tractor slowed to a stop, its engine rumbling on a slow ticker. The cab door clicked open.

"*Jambo* . . . for the *Tillik Sau* . . . " Berry's voice rang out loud and slightly nervously. From outside, one of the guards replied, asked a question in turn, and Berry answered.

Cord glanced at Saat. The Moyallan was leaning forward, straining to hear, his broad mouth closed in a hard, anxious line. The rumble of voices continued for a moment then suddenly the cab door closed, the creak of the barrier pole being raised reached their ears, the tractor grated into gear and they were moving again.

"Ah . . . " David Saat released his breath in a long sigh and wiped the beaded sweat from his forehead. As the vehicle lumbered on, he reached out and slid the compartment door open again. "You did well, Berry," he admitted grudgingly. "Watch your rear view mirrors carefully — I want you to stop again as soon as we are out of sight of that hut."

"All right." Berry's voice was shaky and he didn't turn his head. "What's the idea?"

"I was wondering myself," mused Cord.

"Something I want done," said Saat blandly, but hunching back on his heels in a way which showed he would brook no argument. "By now they will have used that telephone to report we are on our way. If we have to leave this place quickly later, I would prefer the line cut and no risk of other complications."

A few hundred yards on, the track

dipped as it skirted a fold in the ground, a mere suggestion of a hillock crowned by a thick patch of thornbush. Berry licked his lips, checked his mirrors again, then pulled in. Immediately, two of the askaris squeezed their way out of the compartment, dropped from the cab's passenger door to the ground, and almost at once had vanished from sight.

They were gone no longer than it took Cord to smoke his way half-through one of Saat's cigarettes. When they returned, they swung aboard without a word. But one of them drew a finger lightly across his throat in answer to Saat's unspoken question.

"It was necessary," said Saat apologetically as he saw the look of angered understanding in Cord's eyes. "Unpleasant perhaps, but necessary." He cleared his throat awkwardly. "How long now till we are there?"

"Fifteen minutes or so," answered Berry woodenly. He muttered a curse to himself as the sun's glare hit his eyes and adjusted the position of the cab's big, tinted windscreen visor. "Do I keep driving?"

"Straight on in," agreed Cord, with a rasping edge to his voice. "We've had enough of stopping." As they lurched forward again, he scrambled into the cab, gestured for one of the askaris to pass him over the walkie-talkie, and poked its aerial out of the passenger window. It was time to call Duvert, to make sure the Marchetti was airborne and ready.

The Frenchman's voice answered almost immediately. The Marchetti was maintaining position roughly ten miles west of Lake Calu, flying at 15,000 feet.

"Then better start drifting over this way," Cord advised him. "Our ETA is a quarter of an hour from now. Everything okay?"

"Everything — except that my passenger has been sick and would prefer to walk," Duvert's voice cracked cheerfully. "We will be on call when you need us. And, M'sieu Cord — *nakutakia ushindi*. Out."

Saat chuckled. "He wishes us success — though the accent is abominable, even worse than your own."

Cord smiled bleakly, his mind busy with the whole of what had to be done ahead. One error, one crack in the bluff, and the consequences would be sudden and fatal. At least there was still no more than a suspicion of a light breeze in the air — if things stayed that way, as he'd been close to praying they would ever since El Wabir, they had a good chance. A good chance, provided Duvert could locate the Sanctuary camp first time, at the right time.

The minutes ticked by, the tractor swayed on, and the hills began to close in around them, close in with a familiar outline. The gradually tightening expression on Berry's face gave him all the confirmation he needed. He nudged Saat.

"Coming up soon."

Saat nodded, leaning back towards the hatchway, and spoke quietly to the bunched askaris. Whatever he said, they seemed to find it amusing. As he finished, two of them — a different pair from the men who had dealt with the guard post — squeezed their way forward.

"Ready," reported Saat briefly. "How far to go?"

Berry cleared his throat dry with nervous tension. "You'll see the huts once we get past that rise on ahead. From here we've got maybe a quarter mile to travel."

"And no sentries — you're sure?" insisted Cord.

"Not till we reach the valley. Then one at the entrance and one up above." The Mid-Con man swallowed as he watched Saat go very deliberately through the motions of checking the magazine he had just fed into the loading socket of a Patchet gun. "Look, both of you, I — I've done my bit. Just remember if — well, remember Jean is in there somewhere."

Cord looked at him for a moment and nodded his understanding. "Slow down just before we pass the rise," he instructed. "Then keep going slowly the rest of the way, but not so slow it attracts attention."

Berry obeyed to the letter. As the tractor came close in under the rise its speed dropped to a walking pace.

"*Sasa* . . . " David Saat jerked his head at the two waiting askaris. They moved along the broad cab to the passenger door, opened it, and jumped down, breaking into a run the moment their feet hit the ground. Cord closed the door again and reached for the walkie-talkie as the tractor's speed increased a little and they turned into the wide mouth of the main valley.

The dead-end canyon and its huts were ahead. In a moment or two Darrald would be told that his visitors were arriving. He flicked the walkie-talkie switch to 'send'.

★ ★ ★

The guard on the hillside above the Sanctuary camp waved lazily to his comrade below as the six-wheeler came into view. It was a familiar enough sight for both of them and he yawned, tired of this boring duty among the hot rocks, resigned to the fact that the sun had to travel another two slow hours across the sky before he was relieved.

Down below, his companion didn't bother to move as the tractor lumbered past into the mouth of the blank-walled valley and on towards the huts placed so close under the rock face at its far end. The *Tillik Sau*'s guests were expected, there had been a fuss of preparation all morning, and a cluster of men were already waiting curiously around the hut which served as camp headquarters.

"About a dozen of them there," muttered Berry, continuing his tonelessly resigned commentary while he drove. "One or two others hanging about."

Crouched low on the bench seat, close by the passenger door, Cord grimaced. "How many are armed?"

"A few." Berry sucked his teeth nervously. "Some more coming out of the headquarters hut now. Three of them — one a European."

"Darrald?"

"No . . . " Berry frowned. "Looks more like Sydney Holt, from the chemical plant. He comes up now and again when there are transport problems to sort out."

Cord nodded curtly. "I want them to come to us. Stop about a hundred yards from the huts — make it look natural, but with my side of the cab nearest them."

"All right." The man glanced at him briefly. "Then what?"

"Just keep your head down." Cord reached for the door handle as the tractor began to slow and Berry swung the steering wheel. It turned, the gear lever flicked into neutral, and they came to a halt. Cord pushed the door open, swung himself out, and dropped to the ground. He landed catstyle, saw the three men who'd been walking towards the vehicle, and pulled himself erect.

"Cord — " Sydney Holt came to a startled halt in mid-stride, a scant thirty feet away. He gestured to the men at his side and their hands flew to the holstered pistols at their waists. The muzzles swung up, ready.

"Don't," said Cord in a steady voice which somehow came despite the tension jangling every nerve in his body. "I came to give you a chance." He looked past the trio, saw the cluster of men by the hut were shifting uneasily, knowing something was wrong but still uncertain what they should do.

"You damned fool." Holt's flabby red face twisted into something close to a pitying snarl. He started to turn, his mouth opening.

"Wait — I didn't come alone." Cord waved one arm above his head, praying the two askaris were in position. For a moment Holt hesitated — and it was enough. Over at the rear of the little valley, high above the rock face, a blue Very flare burst in the sky and started to fall, burning brightly. Lower down, near the entrance, a second flare, red this time, exploded a second later.

At the huts, the men were already scattering in confusion. Holt's face twitched in frantic indecision then he let out an animal-like cry and began running back the way he'd come. The two Africans, abandoned, reacted more slowly. One stood bewildered, as if fascinated by the burning flares. The other fired wildly, the bullet whining off the tractor's cab.

Cord threw himself flat, rolling, as the gun barked again — and the man had no third chance. Saat's Patchet hammered from the cab's door and the khaki figure jerked and fell. His companion, forced to life, tried to run but tumbled as the rest of the Patchet's magazine kicked the dust around him. David Saat swung down from the cab, the askaris piling out fast behind him, spreading out as they came.

From the rock at the valley entrance a single shot smashed the tractor's windscreen. It was answered from higher up, and Darrald's sentry crashed down from his post. But the men at the huts were what mattered now — already the first ragged firing had begun, building in intensity by the second. An askari, running to a fresh position by the tractor's radiator, seemed to trip, went sprawling, and didn't pick himself up.

Two fresh Very flares burst in the sky — and Cord ignored the firing, straining his ears for another sound, his eyes for the one sight that mattered.

He saw it first, while the firing redoubled, echoing against the valley's sides. The Marchetti, one moment an indistinct speck in the sky, the next a rapidly approaching silhouette, came in fast and low, heading up the main valley like some avenging dart. Cord winced at the sight as it banked for the Sanctuary base's narrow entrance, his nails digging into the palms of his hands as it howled a scant three hundred feet overhead. If Duvert didn't start climbing . . .

Suddenly, as if in answer, the nose came up, the engine howled on maximum revs . . . and as the Marchetti clawed for height two long black shapes tumbled from its underside, falling towards the huts. As the plane cleared the top of the cliff by little more than its own height, the cylinders landed together, close by the headquarters building. Two soft explosions, and a dense purple fog began jetting, to spread like an impenetrable, inky curtain, billowing out to swallow from sight everything it met.

There were shouts from the huts, the pattern of firing grew broken — and already the three askaris detailed to the task were at work with the spring projectors, simple tube-like contraptions which could be fired bazooka-style from the shoulder. The projectors twanged steadily, hurling their little smoke-gas cartridges in a curving arc into the huts, where they popped and burst to add to the quickly thickening fog of purple — a fog lapping out until it met the sides of the narrow valley then, trapped, swirling in growing density.

The Marchetti was coming back, flying higher, circling overhead. The loudhailer barked to life, bellowing above the throttled-back engine.

"*Weka bunduki hapa . . . Una dakaki moya tu. Njoo hapa upesi . . . njoo hapa upesi . . .*" The rasping warning was enough to inject a fresh terror into any man already coughing and struggling in that blinding purple cloud. He had a minute in which to lay down his arms and come out. A minute if he wanted to live — it was a travesty of the truth, but a frightened man, a man who had every reason to believe that he was already trapped, was unlikely to sit down and try and exercise in cold rationalising.

But some, at least, required a little more convincing. A harsh, methodical anvil-beat clattered from the left fringe of the cloud as a heavy machine-gun opened up, firing in a blind, seeking arc which was too close to its target for comfort. Cord hand-signalled, the three spring-projectors swung and thumped in unison, and a moment later the cloud sprang up in a fresh intensity around the spot.

The machine-gun fired another ragged burst, then fell silent.

"Talos?" Saat crossed towards him at a fast crouch. The spring projectors were still thumping, the rest of Saat's little squad answering the rapidly fading shots from that swirling mist.

"Now," nodded Cord.

Saat flicked a whistle from one pocket of his tunic, blew a long, single note and the askaris ceased fire. They'd been well rehearsed — as one man, they pulled on their smoke masks and began to spread out into an almost ludicrously thin line, advancing slowly towards the fringe of the waiting cloud.

The firing had stopped there too, and the Marchetti came back, circling again, the loudhailer reiterating its warning.

The words were still echoing when the first figure blundered out from the cloud, eyes streaming, arms waving frantically above his head. The nearest askari, grotesque in his smoke-mask, let the man come a few steps further then clipped him neatly behind the ear with the barrel of his rifle.

Wincing, Cord saw two other faint-hearts come out further along the line and be similarly dealt with. But the next man to emerge, heading straight for him, a tall, snarling figure with a Sten gun still clenched in his hands, made him change his mind. While the man still stood undecided, the Sten swinging blindly, Cord dodged behind him, reversed the Neuhausen, and knocked him out with the butt.

The trickle soon became a flood of frightened, blundering would-be prisoners and, the critical moments over, their reception could be eased. A perfunctory search, and one by one they were herded back to squat miserably under a solitary guard. A quick exchange of shots from the cliff behind the huts lasted a few seconds then died away as some hardier individual who'd tried to find another way out was turned back.

He ignored the confusion, watching and waiting until, at last, he spotted Sydney Holt. The plant manager stumbled out with his head down, a handkerchief clutched over his mouth and his eyes red, watering slits. He tripped, fell, then scrambled to his feet and tried to peer around. Cord closed the gap between them at a fast-striding lope while Holt waited as if suddenly rooted by his irresolution, his empty hands held out in hopeful appeal.

"All right, you're safe enough." Cord grabbed the plant manager roughly by the arm and dragged him further back. "What's happened to the girl — and where's Darrald?"

"They're — they're not here." Holt coughed and rubbed his eyes as if he would never stop. "Cord, I need help, a doctor — "

"You'll live," said Cord harshly. "All you've had is a dose of Technicolor tear-smoke."

"Tear-smoke . . . " Holt cursed weakly in a blend of relief and despair. "You mean it was just a trick, a stupid — " he broke off, coughing — "a stupid, schoolboy trick?"

"It worked," snapped Cord. "Come on, Holt. Where are they?"

"You've slipped up." An expression of unholy satisfaction crossed the man's face. "The girl was moved back to the house last night. She's still there."

"And the other two?" Cord's grip tightened on his shoulder.

"You — you came in too soon." Holt chose his words more wanly. "I got a message to come here and keep the Congo party occupied for a spell. Darrald and Nyeme were going to be delayed — some snag about a shipment

305

coming in. They'd radioed a query and were waiting for the answer." He screwed his eyes tight again and asked anxiously, "Cord, you're sure it's only tear-smoke?"

"Yes." Cord swore bitterly to himself. Behind them the mopping up was ending, the purple vapour was already beginning to thin on the breeze. Saat's men had their prisoners bunched together now, Duvert's Marchetti was circling lazily high above their heads, there was no doubt about their victory. Yet Holt's news meant the job was still far from over. He shoved the plant manager along to join the rest of the captives, let a grinning, limping askari relieve him of his charge, then hurried towards the tractor.

Hal Berry met him halfway, the eagerness on his face giving way to something close to fear as he saw Cord's expression.

"Where is she?" he asked. The nasal voice rose louder. "Where's Jean — what's happened to her?"

"She's not here." Cord tried to brush past him.

"Not — " Berry's mouth fell open. "Look, I did what you asked — "

"But she's not here. She's at the house or she was." Cord shouldered him aside, heading for the tractor. The askari wounded in the first exchange of fire was propped against one wheel, his uniform soaked down the right side by a dark bloodstain, his face the colour of slate.

Berry caught up with him again as he started to climb into the cab. "Cord, you promised — "

"She's with Darrald and Nyeme," rapped Cord, cutting him short. "They were delayed. That means by now they've probably found the guard post at the entrance unmanned — "

"Or the guards." Berry groaned in a despair of understanding. "Then they'd — " he broke off, biting his lip.

Cord nodded brusquely. "They'd head back. Don't be a fool, Berry.

They need her more than ever now as a possible bargaining card." He swung into the cab and grabbed the walkie-talkie from the floor.

"What can you do?" asked Berry despairingly, climbing up alongside. "Look, if — "

"If you hadn't got into the mess in the first place they wouldn't have her now," Cord reminded him brutally. "John Spence is watching the house. We'll find out what he knows first."

Duvert answered the radio call with only a second's delay, his voice gaily confident.

"From here it looks good," he reported. "All over, eh, m'sieu — or is there more I can do? Over."

Cord thumbed the switch. "Darrald isn't here. Raise Spence and tell him to stay put — tell him I want to know what's been happening at his end."

They waited, Berry rocking gently to and fro on the bench seat, fists clenched, his eyes staring at the little set. The cab door swung open and

David Saat scrambled up beside them, his face glistening with sweat. He barely glanced at Berry and grinned across at Cord.

"This is a day I will long remember," he said happily. "We have done well — twenty of them rounded up, another three dead. Yet, scratches apart, only two of my men were wounded." One hand thumped the tractor's steering wheel for added emphasis. "And three of these huts, the largest, are filled to the roof with enough arms and ammunition for a complete regiment, maybe more!"

"Congratulations," grated Berry.

Saat gave the man a tolerant shrug. "I haven't forgotten your sister, Berry. Or that we have still other business to finish. But I wouldn't worry too much."

"Want me to thank you?" asked Berry cynically.

The radio crackled, and Cord waved them to silence.

"Spence is still watching the house,"

reported Duvert briskly. "He says a car left there about an hour ago and has not yet returned. He suggests he should move in now."

Cord rubbed a hand through his short, dark hair as the message ended. Darrald might have done either of two things — turned back when he reached the Sanctuary's entrance and found the guards gone, or kept on until he had a distant view of the attack on the camp. But which? The first possibility was infinitely the more dangerous.

"How long would it take to drive back to Darrald's place from the gate?" he asked Saat.

The Moyallan frowned and shrugged. "It is no road for breaking records. Half an hour — no quicker unless they had wings."

"Unless they had wings — " Cord stared at him for a moment, then thumbed the send button again. "Duvert, could you land and take off from here, then set the plane down near Darrald's house?"

Listening, Saat gave a plaintive groan. There was a long silence from the Marchetti's pilot and when he answered the gaiety was gone from his voice.

"I can try. What do I tell Spence?"

That was harder. Cord pursed his lips. "Tell him Darrald and Nyeme were probably in that car and should be heading back now. Tell him — " he drew a deep breath, " — tell him if he can go in fast and out again faster to do it. The choice is his."

There was another silence, broken only by the drone of the plane overhead. Then Duvert answered, a touch of dry humour in his voice.

"He says affirmative. I should be with you shortly — I think."

8

PAUL DUVERT took his time — and none of the watchers on the ground could blame him. Three times the blue Marchetti circled low, at dangerously close to stalling speed, tricycle undercarriage wound down. Once he seemed on the final stage of landing, then at the last moment the engine sang in full throttle as he broke off the approach.

But finally he committed himself. The Marchetti sank down, touched, and came bumping crazily along the scrub laced surface. Wings rocking wildly, it skidded round to a halt with its port wheel jammed against a patch of thorn. Cord and Saat raced over, to find Duvert climbing shakily from the cabin. He dropped to the ground, looked at them, and forced a grin.

"Something tells me I am a lucky

man," he admitted wryly, then thumbed towards the plane. "Inspector, I think your sergeant should be told to open his eyes now."

The askari sergeant emerged slowly, shook his head in a daze, then swallowed and made a hasty exit towards the nearest clump of bush.

"You had us worried," said Cord, relief in his voice.

"I had myself worried, m'sieu," agreed Duvert. He glanced at the undercarriage, frowned, and crossed over to inspect it more closely. When he came back, he seemed satisfied.

"The strut is damaged a little," he shrugged. "But it should hold for a time."

"Then we'll start whenever you're ready," nodded Cord.

"All I must do is speak with my sergeant — " began Saat.

"A moment, Inspector . . ." Duvert looked back along the way he'd landed and winced. "You and I perhaps, M'sieu Cord. But no more.

I have no urgent desire to be with the angels. She came down, so she should manage up again — but I need minimum take-off weight." He saw the expression on Saat's face and shook his head. "Already, before I came down, I jettisoned as much gasoline as is wise."

Saat scowled unhappily, but there could be no argument about the situation. He rubbed a hand across his chin and came up with a fresh suggestion.

"I can take one of Darrald's jeeps and follow with a couple of men — we might arrive in time to be useful." He glanced back at the huts where his captives were now sitting in two long lines on the ground, under watchful guard. "My sergeant can take care of things here — there may be a few stray patrols among the hills, but little more."

"It sounds sensible," agreed Cord.

A trio of askaris helped them free the Marchetti and turn her round. Duvert climbed aboard, Cord followed, and as they strapped themselves down the pilot reached out briefly to touch the St. Christopher medallion he had hanging on the instrument panel. He looked at Cord and grinned.

"Siai-Marchetti, a most reliable firm, lay down a minimum take-off run of seven hundred and twenty feet for this air-craft, m'sieu. I reckon we have six hundred — but then, their figures are usually conservatively safe."

"We'll find out," said Cord grimly. "Any more items like that you can keep till we get up there."

Duvert nodded, hummed quietly to himself, signalled the men on the ground to stand clear, and pressed the self-starter. The engine fired, its note rose to a noisy roar, and the constant speed propeller became a shimmering, whirling disc. Duvert was still humming, but his face became set and tense as he edged the throttle further forward and the Marchetti strained against its wheel-brakes. Then with a brief glance at Cord, he jammed the throttle fully forward and they were rolling.

Heaving, lurching, the plane gathered speed and the ground began to flicker past. Cord drew a deep breath as Duvert heaved the control column back as far as it would come and for a brief moment they seemed to hesitate between ground and air. Then the Marchetti was climbing, the Sanctuary camp below was shrinking to the proportions of a doll's village, the men down there had become the size of ants.

"I will send a personal postcard of congratulation to M'sieu Marchetti, if he exists," murmured Duvert in thankful delight. He levelled out their rate of climb, pushed a switch, then frowned at the instrument panel, where a little red light had begun winking.

"Trouble?" asked Cord.

Duvert flick switched again without replying. The red light stayed winking and he shrugged. "The port landing wheel, the one which was damaged — now

it will not retract, nor will it relock."
He grimaced ruefully. "When we land
it should be interesting. However, as
a consolation, you may smoke now if
you wish, m'sieu."

Somehow, Cord didn't feel in the
mood.

They levelled out completely at five
thousand feet, the engine settled to
a steady quiet note and the airspeed
indicator quivering close to maximum
cruising speed. Duvert thumbed towards
the ground. "The Sanctuary boundary,
near the entry gate — do we follow the
road?"

Cord nodded agreement. "If we spot
that car we're in business."

He looked down and picked out the
hill track, a slender brown bootlace of
a line snaking through the landscape
of scrub and bush below. It was empty
for as far as the eye could see. Either
Darrald was still driving somewhere on
ahead, or . . . He tried the radio, called
Spence, waited, tried again, but there
was no answer.

"Maybe he is still in the house," suggested Duvert. "In his shoes, I would not leave a man to listen on the chance someone calls."

The Marchetti droned on, the track below remained empty, and gradually the hills began to give way to more level terrain. In the distance, the grey, scarred surface of the soda ash lake with its scatter of buildings showed they were coming close to their destination. Duvert's fingers moved lightly over the controls and they banked gently on a new course, following the edge of the hills.

"We will be near the *Tillik Sau*'s place soon," he reminded, glancing at Cord.

"I'll try Spence again." Cord went through the routine, but there was still no answer and his fears kept growing. "All right, circle the house once, not too low. Then make it look as though we're heading on for El Wabir."

"But instead, we land." Duvert nodded his understanding then murmured, half to himself, "And when we do, *bon chance* to one and all."

From two thousand feet, throttled back, Lucas Darrald's white-walled home looked more than ever a painstaking replica of some nineteenth century fortress. Yet it seemed peaceful enough — almost too peaceful. Nothing moved as they circled, seeing the police Land-Rover stopped just outside the main door. The usual assortment of farm vehicles were parked at the rear, but there was no sign of Darrald's white Mercedes.

"Enough?" queried Duvert.

Reluctantly, he nodded and the plane banked away towards the east.

Five minutes later, after Duvert had doubled back and had treated his passenger to a nerve-racking display of precision zero-altitude flying, they made a neat, surprisingly uncomplicated dead-engine belly landing in a maize field behind a rise of ground.

The Marchetti's propeller was smashed, the tip of one wing had disappeared, and the underside of the fuselage looked as if a madman had attacked it with a twenty-pound hammer.

But they were down, intact and, with luck, unseen.

★ ★ ★

Travelling at the fast, crouching pace Cord set from the maize field on was something Duvert found far from pleasant. Panting, badly out of breath, he flopped down thankfully when, at last, they reached the mimosa windbreak overlooking Darrald's house. He pushed a damp lock of hair back from his dripping forehead and groaned.

"What now, m'sieu?"

Cord edged forward beneath the pink blossoms of the hedge and made a careful inspection of what lay ahead. The police Land-Rover remained parked beside the archway leading to the building's central courtyard and everything still seemed peaceful.

Nothing moved on the road, he could see no sign of a dust-cloud which might tell of an approaching vehicle.

Vaguely uneasy, he brushed away an ant crawling on his arm and was wriggling back towards Duvert when he saw a movement at the archway. Jean Berry walked out of the big white house, glanced around, then opened the Land-Rover's passenger door and stood there, looking back towards the house as if waiting for someone to follow.

A grunt by his side showed his companion had also seen her. Duvert asked hopefully, "Everything is okay, eh?"

"Maybe." Cord hesitated, then nodded. "I think so. Let's go."

They left cover and walked boldly across the grassy slope towards the house. The girl saw them coming and after a moment raised one arm in a slow wave of welcome. There was a strange, indefinable weariness in the gesture and she stayed where she was.

More uneasy than ever but committed now, Cord kept on. By the time he was close enough to see the tense pallor of her face it was too late even if he'd wanted to turn back.

"Welcome again, Mr Cord." Richarn Nyeme stepped out from the shadow of the archway, hands in the pockets of his twill slacks, a patronising, self-satisfied grin on his thin face. "No — " he gave a quick warning shake of his head as Duvert reached towards the pistol at his waist. "Don't be foolish."

A bulky Moyallan in slacks and ragged singlet moved just behind Nyeme, an automatic carbine at the ready. Cord sighed, raised his hands, and, as Duvert followed his example, saw Jean Berry regarding them in silent, downcast apology.

"Nicely done, Miss Berry," congratulated Nyeme sardonically. He chose a careful path which didn't mask the waiting carbine, stepped behind his two prisoners, and removed their guns. "You were most co-operative."

"I didn't have much choice." Her voice was low and bitter. "Talos — "

"She wishes to tell you that her friend Spence is sitting with a pistol muzzle against his ear," murmured Nyeme with a cold amusement. "And so she decided it was best to co-operate. As for how we knew you were coming, blame a well-meaning field hand who ran all the way with the news that an aeroplane had crashed. It was not hard to understand." His face hardened into something close to a snarl. "This time you have not been quite clever enough. Move — the girl will lead the way."

They obeyed, Nyeme and his carbine guard bringing up the rear. Cord swore softly as they passed the dust-stained white Mercedes drawn up inside the archway's shelter, a shimmer of heat still rising from its radiator. Across the brick-paved courtyard, through the same little doorway as before — they stopped outside Nyeme's office, he tapped lightly on the door, opened it, and gestured them in.

The three people in the room regarded them with very different expressions. John Spence sat in a straight-backed chair in the middle of the floor, his lined face grim with despair, blood still trickling from a smashed lip. Behind him, Lucas Darrald's dark piercing eyes glowed angrily as he sighted Cord. But the small, thick-set figure said nothing, the gun in his hand remaining trained on the back of Spence's head.

That left Paula Darrald. Dressed like Jean Berry in bush shirt and slacks, her fair hair slightly tousled, she stirred almost lazily in her chair by the window, her face expressionless. Cord felt a brief upsurge of hope as he saw the way she glanced quickly to make sure no other eyes were on her and gave an almost imperceptible shake of her head.

"Looks like I made a mess of things," said Spence thickly in a grey, unhappy voice.

"The stumbling amateur," agreed Nyeme with cynical cruelty. "But you are no amateur, Mr Cord." He bared his teeth in a fractional mirthless smile. "It seems Lucas and I were wrong about you, badly wrong."

"That was our mistake," growled Darrald heavily, his leathery square-jawed face twitching. He nodded towards the guard and the man quietly closed the door, taking up a position beside it, the carbine held ready. "Coming here at this time was yours, Cord."

"Maybe." Cord regarded them bleakly. "What matters the Sanctuary's finished, Darrald. No more *Tillik Sau* stuff, no more big deal business — "

Darrald took three steps across the room and cut him short with a powerful, back-handed blow across the mouth. It stung, and Cord felt the salt taste of blood in his lips. He guessed he'd just sampled a little of the treatment already dished out to Spence.

* * *

"Nothing's finished," declared Darrald violently. "We need a new base, but that's something I've been prepared for as insurance — we'll be back in business soon enough. People like you are temporary setbacks, nothing more."

"Lucas — " Nyeme cleared his throat and glanced significantly at his watch.

Darrald nodded and beckoned towards Paula. "You'd better see to your things now, girl. We'll check on the truck."

"All right." She rose lazily, brushed past Spence's chair, and stopped for a moment beside Jean Berry. The two girls, so opposite in appearance, looked at each other in silence for a moment then Paula shrugged deliberately and moved on towards the door.

"We will be back soon," promised Nyeme meaningly, opening the door. He thumbed towards the guard. "For all of your benefits, he has orders to shoot to kill."

Darrald grunted briefly, let his daughter go out first, then followed. Nyeme looked around again, smiled that same cold, humourless smile, and closed the door behind him as he left.

"And that's that," said Cord ruefully. He reached one hand towards the cheroots in his top pockets, saw the carbine jerk in his direction, and didn't complete the movement. "How do you feel, Jean?"

She walked slowly to the chair vacated by Paula and sat down with a shaky sigh. "All right. But — Talos, I'm sorry about what happened out there."

"What else could you have done?" murmured Duvert. The Frenchman looked around with a glum expectancy, then contemplated the collection of weapons decorating the opposite wall. "If Darrald was holding a gun against my head I hope my friends would do exactly as he asked."

"That's how it was," said Spence miserably. "We came in, we dealt wi' a couple o' guards, got the girls, found the papers you wanted, an' then — then we walked straight into Darrald and Nyeme on the way out. They'd another couple o' men with them."

"What about the askaris?" asked Cord grimly.

Spence shook his head. "One dead, the other poor devil knocked on the head and locked up somewhere."

"And the question now is what will happen to us," muttered Duvert. He remembered the girl and flushed. "*Idiot* . . . I am sorry, Jean."

She gave him a slow, grave smile. "I didn't imagine they were going to invite us to tea, Paul." Her attention switched back to Cord. "Is Hal all right?"

He nodded, and she gave a sigh of relief.

"They must have made that return strip in a really steaming hurry," mused Cord. He stopped, glanced at the stony-faced native by the doorway, and chose his words carefully. "Well, I hope someone else is still playing happy families for us."

Jean stared at him for a moment then understood. "She is. Things worked out that way — but sometimes you can't do much if you haven't the right cards."

Out of the corner of his eye, Cord watched Duvert move casually nearer to the opposite wall, edging towards one of the heavy clubs. But the guard had seen him too.

"*Hapana* . . . " the Moyallan jumped forward, rammed the muzzle of the carbine against Duvert's stomach, and pushed him back. Then, with a scowl, he returned to his post by the door.

Cord relaxed again with a sigh. Duvert had meant well, but it had been the kind of crazy, hopeful action which might have ended in the room being sprayed with bullets. They waited in silence for some moments, then there was a quiet tap on the door. The guard opened it cautiously. Paula Darrald came in, a softly tanned leather jacket over her shirt and slacks, looked at them without expression, then turned and spoke to the guard in a low, quiet voice. He gave a slow, stubborn shake of his head and she moved away, frowning a little.

"In to say goodbye?" queried Cord cheerfully.

"Something like that." Her back to the door, she let one side of the jacket swing open. Cord had to fight to keep his voice level as he saw the Neuhausen pushed into the waistband of her slacks and read the message in her eyes.

"How long have we got?" he asked.

"Only till they come back." She took another step nearer. "They're loading a truck, then we're on our way. My — my father thinks it would be too risky to try the airstrip."

"Maybe they could use some help," suggested Jean Berry hopefully, glancing significantly towards the guard.

"He won't move," answered Paula briefly.

"A pity." Cord gauged the gap

between them, the seconds he'd need to reach the Neuhausen, how fast the man at the doorway would react. If Paula had — but there was no use dwelling on that one. The tall slim girl was trapped in a crossfire of loyalties and emotions, one in which few people could be counted on to do more than surrender to circumstances.

The door swung open again and he gave a half-suppressed groan as Darrald and Nyeme came in, the opportunity vanished with their return. The *Tillik Sau* had a satchel slung over one shoulder on a long strap, and Nyeme carried a duplicate of the guard's automatic carbine.

"*Endelea . . . sasa . . .* " Darrald jerked his head at the guard and the man grinned then went out. "Paula — "

"Yes?" She turned only her head towards him.

"Time to go."

She moistened her lips. "I'm not coming."

"What?" Darrald sounded as though he couldn't believe his ears.

"I'm staying." The words came low but firmly and she glanced back at Cord in a desperate appeal.

Nyeme saw the glance, somehow sensed the separate tension between Cord and the girl. He crossed over at lightning speed, the carbine's muzzle rested against her back, and then he glared over her shoulder at Cord.

"Move back," he grated, then, as Cord reluctantly obeyed, he added, "Lucas, she's your daughter — and I think you should see if she's hiding anything under that coat."

"Hiding — " Darrald scowled, mystified, sighed heavily, and moved forward. "Turn round, girl." He gripped her by one shoulder, swung her round none too gently, found the gun, and took it from her waistband. His voice sank to a deep, low growl. "What the hell's going on, Paula?"

"I can tell you," said Cord quietly. He ignored Nyeme and went on. "She's had enough, Darrald."

"Enough?" Lucas Darrald sucked in his lips, still shaken. "Paula — "

She shook her head, avoiding his gaze.

Nyeme moved back a little towards the door, his eyes suddenly bright with suspicion. "For just how long has Paula 'had enough', Mr Cord?" he asked with a deadly silkiness. "Long enough to explain why you achieved so much progress in a very short time?"

"Richarn — " Darrald's head snapped towards him. "I'll handle it."

"Maybe you shouldn't," declared Nyeme grimly. "She is your own blood."

"So was Frank." The words blurted from Paula's lips. "But that didn't stop you letting him be killed, did it, father? I've loathed the rest, but this — "

Lucas Darrald seemed to recoil from the agony in her voice. "What — look, girl, what madness is this?" He swallowed hard, his face pale. "There was a plane crash, Frank died in it, I wasn't even here at the time. Am I to blame?"

Ignored, almost forgotten, John Spence rose unsteadily from his chair. "She knows the truth, Darrald," he said quietly. "All of us do. You and that attendant devil of yours decided that plane had to crash to get rid of Cord's friend — and you wouldn't even let your son get in the way of achieving it."

"Liar." With a growl, Nyeme swung the barrel of the carbide. It took Spence across the face and he staggered back, tripped over the chair, and crashed to the floor. He lay there for a moment then slowly dragged himself upright, shaking his head in a daze of pain.

"There is no time to this," said Nyeme urgently. "Lucas, time is what they are seeking — there are bound to be police on their way from the Sanctuary. If she won't come then — leave her."

Slowly, Darrald shook his head. "I want to know what she means about

Frank." He laid a hand on Paula's arm then drew it back again as she stared down at it. "All right, Paula, I had to get rid of a spy in the last trainee group and we didn't know who he was — just that he existed, that someone had been prowling around. And we — Richarn and I decided the only way was for that plane to crash." He drew a deep breath. "But I didn't know Frank was going to board it. If I had — I'd have stopped him, no matter what it cost."

"Twenty-six men for one," breathed Paul Duvert, a bewildered spectator. "Mon Dieu . . . what kind of people are you?"

"Do you think I liked it?" asked Darrald bitterly. "We'd no choice." He turned back to the girl. "Paula, I didn't know about Frank."

"I believe you, Darrald — as far as you go." The unexpected conviction in Cord's voice demanded attention. "But how much do you know yourself?" He saw the look gathering on Nyeme's face and warned quickly, "If you want to hear me out, tell your hired help to behave."

"He will." Darrald grated the words. "Go on, Cord. But I'm losing patience."

"I'll keep it short," agreed Cord grimly. "You went off to the coast so that you'd be nowhere near at the time it happened, and you left Nyeme to fix the details."

"With Johann Balder," said Nyeme quickly, almost nervously. "He was paid well to do it. I was far away too — the *Tillik Sau* knows it."

Cord noticed the sudden change in the way he named Darrald but let it pass. He had a more important path to follow. "Darrald, if you'd heard what Hal Berry told me last night you'd realise differently. Nyeme was at the airstrip with Frank that day. He let Frank get on the plane. He saw it crash. Then he warned Berry and Johann Balder to keep their mouths shut and went away. Where did he tell you he'd been?"

"The Sanctuary . . . " Very slowly,

Darrald turned and stared at Nyeme without really seeing him then gave a sigh. "Richarn — "

"They're lying — to confuse you," insisted Nyeme with an almost hysterical urgency. "If we don't go soon — "

"My brother saw you. He told me." Jean Berry met Nyeme's gaze across the room and refused to be beaten down. "Mr Darrald, did he ever prove he was at the Sanctuary?"

"No." Lucas Darrald still had the Neuhausen in his hand. All expression drained from his face and his voice became hard and flat. "He didn't. But he told me Balder and that native Wani had to be killed because they were wanting more money or would talk."

"Talk maybe," agreed Cord. "But not to the police — to you, Darrald. About what really happened."

A faint click sounded. Nyeme had slid the carbine's selector lever to automatic. "That gun," he said, a sudden sharp edge honed into his tones. "Put it down, Lucas — down, or you will not be the first to die."

Slowly, wordlessly, Darrald laid the pistol on the desk then moved back at the carbine's urging.

"You, just you — " said Paula Darrald in a whisper.

"Just me," agreed Nyeme huskily. "Frank wanted to fly to the coast that day, to join his father, as a surprise. I said I'd take him." His face twisted briefly. "It was a good reason to be at the airstrip, to fix the charges — simple little barb metric devices, two of them, in the controls. They are built to explode when an aircraft reaches a certain height, with reduced air pressure actuating the triggers. There was plenty of time, and we would be in the air ourselves, far away, before the transport took off."

"But something went wrong," prodded Cord, playing for time, fervently hoping for some miracle to remove the menace of that carbine's mouth.

"Something went wrong," agreed Nyeme tonelessly. "A fuel-line fault in our plane, right on take-off. Frank said he'd hitch a lift in the transport, insisted on going on it." His lips pressed close together for an instant. "Yes, I could have told him about those charges, that he was going to his death. But what would he have done?"

"Stopped it happening," grunted John Spence, dabbing a handkerchief to his face. "Frank was no butcher."

"He was a fool," snapped Nyeme, defensively. "When we were children together he was always the same — soft, foolish. If that plane had been allowed to fly, if the spy aboard had got free, we were finished."

"You were friends once," said Lucas Darrald in an old man's voice. "Richarn, you — you just let him go?"

Nyeme licked his lips and nodded, as if not trusting himself to answer. He began to edge towards the door — then suddenly his eyes widened, his mouth began to open.

Lucas Darrald pulled the ancient spear from its wall mounting in no seeming hurry, with a final deliberate purpose. The carbine began to stutter as his arm drew back for the throw and he staggered as the first bullets tore into him. But his arm still came forward, the spear flew even as he fell, and its sharp, terrible blade raked across Nyeme's right shoulder before it stuck in the wood of the door, its shaft quivering.

The carbine stopped and Nyeme's left hand went up to dab in something like wonder at the red stain of blood already spreading from the cut in his shirt. Then, still watchful, he reached behind him, opened the door, stepped out, and closed it.

The spell was broken.

One glance at Darrald was enough. The *Tillik Sau* was dead, a whole pattern of bullet holes punched through the front of his chest. Paula dropped on her knees beside the dead man, already knowing, looking up at Cord with eyes drained of every emotion except a blind, empty shock. He touched her gently on the shoulder then moved quickly to the desk, grabbed the Neuhausen, and headed for the door. Duvert was right behind him. The young pilot stopped to wrench the spear from the wooden panel, hefted it grimly, and nodded.

The corridor outside was empty. Cord sprinted along and out into the central courtyard, saw the Mercedes still lying silent and deserted, and waved Duvert to follow him towards the rear of the building.

Another dash across the brick paving and back along the corridor brought them into the kitchen quarters, equally deserted, the cooking stoves cold, dirty dishes piled on a table. There was a broad door at the back, locked, and no sign of the key. Two shots from the Neuhausen smashed the lock and they bounded out into the kitchen yard.

A truck stood about fifty yards away, its cab doors opened, three natives pawing feverishly among the packs of stores piled inside its platform. They turned as Cord and Duvert sprinted towards them and one of them, the singlet-clad guard from Nyeme's office, dived for his gun.

Cord dropped to a crouch, sighted using both hands, and squeezed the trigger. The Neuhausen barked again and the guard crumpled while his two companions threw themselves bodily over the side of the truck and ran, looting forgotten, their only aim now to put distance between themselves and the house. He let them go, while Duvert dropped the spear in exchange for the guard's carbine. The truck's cab was empty, the only sound in the yard was the whispering wind.

"*Doucement*," murmured Duvert more or less to himself. "He has to be here somewhere, m'sieu. If he has known this place since a child there are many places he could hide."

Cord thought of a child, of two children. He knew where he had to go — and, equally suddenly, why.

"Go back to the others, then keep

an eye open for David Saat coming," he said quietly.

Duvert hesitated, then nodded and went back into the building. Once he'd gone, Cord fed a fresh magazine into the Neuhausen and was ready.

★ ★ ★

It was cool in the shadows of the big centre courtyard, and Cord's footsteps sounded loud as he walked towards the base of the one-time bell-tower. The door was ajar, and it creaked open as he pushed against the wood. Inside, all he could see was a dark gloom with a flight of stone stairs winding upwards. He listened, and heard the faint sound of laboured breathing coming from somewhere above his head.

"Nyeme . . . " his voice echoed up the stairway and he waited.

A sudden clatter of metal falling on stone jerked him back against the wall, then the carbine tumbled down the last few steps and landed at his feet.

"Up here, Mr Cord," announced Nyeme's voice, a measure of grim humour injected the slowly spoken words. "Do not worry — it will be quite safe."

He climbed the narrow, twisting stairway, the Neuhausen ready, cobwebs brushing his face, the old, dry smell of the tower in his nostrils. Richarn Nyeme lay on a step halfway up the tower, his back propped against the wall, his legs drawn up under him. One hand rose in a weakly cynical welcome as Cord reached him.

"You, or perhaps Paula Darrald — only two people would have come to this place so quickly," he said unemotionally. "You know why I am here, sitting like this in the dark?"

"I guessed," nodded Cord. "You warned me about those spears."

"The wound can be as small as a pinprick and still be enough," murmured Nyeme. His left hand went up to press against the cut in his shoulder. "My tribe were skilled in their knowledge of poison."

"A doctor — "

"Can you find me one in five minutes?" Nyeme shook his head. "The process is well under way. It is hard to breathe, I have a feeling as if a collar was tightening around my neck." His eyes glinted briefly. "No need for embarrassment, I have no intention of making a dying plea for understanding or any similar crudity. The *Tillik Sau* . . . "

"Dead."

Nyeme sighed, winced, and coughed a little at the effort of drawing breath. "You ruined a rich enterprise, Mr Cord. One that would have given me power . . . at least, eventually."

"That's what you wanted.?"

The Moyallan nodded. Cord saw the eyes close briefly, could hear the shallow breathing quicken. Then Nyeme stirred.

"The last minute or so will be unpleasant, and I would prefer to avoid it," he said carefully. "You have that little gun, Mr Cord — it would be a courtesy if you leave it when you go."

Cord looked down at him for a long moment. Then, wordlessly, he laid the Neuhausen on the step beside the man, turned, went down the stairway, and walked out into the courtyard and its great open roof of blue sky.

The muffled shot reached his ears as he reached the outer archway.

★ ★ ★

By the time David Saat's jeep-load of askaris arrived, ready and eager to take over, there was little left to be done.

"Maybe it is better this way," admitted Saat almost regretfully as he followed Cord back out of the bell tower, the last point on his tour of the house. "There is still the daughter of course, but — " he shrugged " — I have no quarrel with her. She can go."

Cord nodded, satisfied. "What about Hal Berry?"

"That one?" Saat rubbed one foot over the red brick paving and scowled. "He helped when he had little alternative, but not before. There will be charges to answer, a penalty to pay. But I would not feel too sorry for him — he may learn a lesson in the process." He glanced towards the house, where Jean Berry stood quietly waiting. "For his sister's sake, I hope so."

"Duvert has an idea he wants to talk to you about," said Cord almost absently. Duvert had something else too — Darrald's satchel of papers, papers which were going to raise eyebrows in several places when it was realised where the *Tillik Sau*'s arms had been purchased and to whom they'd been sold. "We'll leave most of the records in your hands, and just take a few that are particularly interesting . . . all right?"

"Of course," agreed Saat cheerfully. "For the rest, I will leave it to my superiors to decide. They are going to be particularly interested in the weapons and equipment we have

— ah — acquired. There must be enough stored at the Sanctuary to fight at least a little war."

Cord gave a small smile and looked at his watch. "Mind if I borrow that jeep for a spell? I've a report to radio and something else I'd like to finish."

"Take it," agreed Saat expansively. "I will have a report of my own to write — but it can wait till later, when I am ready to enjoy it."

The jeep's fuel tank was still half-full. Cord climbed aboard, started the motor, looked for a last time at the big white house, and drove away.

★ ★ ★

It was late afternoon when he finally arrived back in El Wabir and steered towards the airstrip. By then, he felt caked in a mixture of dust and sweat, his muscles ached, and the jeep's fuel gauge was reading almost empty. But there was a grin on his face as he saw the big twin-engined Executive Dove which had been Lucas Darrald's now warming up on the runway. His last task lay behind him.

A wounded askari was being loaded aboard the plane, with John Spence one of the helpers. As the stretcher disappeared into the Dove, Spence turned round, saw Cord, waved, and crossed over.

"Man, you've had one or two people worried," declared Spence as he arrived. "Where have you been the last few hours?"

"Just tying up some loose ends," said Cord soothingly. He swung out of the jeep and brushed the worst of the dust from his clothes. "Any problems at this end?"

"None," said the Food and Agriculture man happily. "Paula agreed straight away to young Duvert using the plane. We've put three wounded aboard for Nygall hospital — the askari and two of the others. I can cope wi' the rest."

"Fine." Cord's face twitched a little as he glimpsed David Saat striding towards them from the airstrip office. He had little time left. "And Paula?"

"She's on the plane." Spence rubbed a lean hand along his chin and became more serious. "Jean said she should stay wi' her for a spell, an' I offered to keep an eye on them both. But the girl wants out, right away from it all, so — well, Saat an' I will take care of things for her. Ach, I can't blame her." He studied Cord for a moment and gave a friendly chuckle. "If you want to say goodbye you'd better hurry."

David Saat was drawing near, the fly-whisk swinging from one wrist, a slight frown on his face. Cord slapped the Scot cheerfully on the shoulder and headed for the plane at a fast jog-trot. He swung himself aboard then waited at the doorway until the policeman panted alongside.

"Where have you been?" demanded Saat with a wary suspicion. "I have had men looking for you — "

The Dove's engines died to a purr, and Paul Duvert eased his way through the cabin to the doorway. He stopped and cleared his throat apologetically.

"If we are to reach Nygall by nightfall it is time to go, M'sieu Cord. Otherwise, I cannot guarantee you will connect with that outward flight."

Saat's mouth fell open. "You — you are leaving now? But your luggage and the rest — "

"Duvert collected them." Cord gave a suspicion of a grin as the pilot moved back towards his controls. "I'm finished here."

"There is a reason for this," said Saat with an unhappy foreboding. "But — " his next few words were drowned as the Dove's engines roared. He grimaced and tried again. *Nakutakia heri* . . . good luck."

Cord waved briefly, closed the cabin door, and scrambled forward in the cabin, past the stretchers. The plane was already rolling as he dropped into the vacant seat beside Paula Darrald. She stared at him, bewildered, while he fastened his seat belt.

"Surprised?" he queried.

She nodded, and drew a deep breath as they gathered speed down the runway. They didn't speak again until the Dove was airborne, already climbing over Lake Calu, starting to swing towards the north.

"It's over now, Paula," said Cord understandingly. "Made up your mind what you'll do?"

She relaxed back in her seat, her eyes straying to the window and the shrinking landscape below. "Go back to London, I suppose. For a spell, anyway — until things are sorted out."

"And after that?"

She shrugged. "I don't know."

"There's no hurry about it," he mused. "But I happen to know a good cure for the way you feel. If you were interested."

Paula Darrald said nothing for a moment, then a slow smile began to build in the corners of her mouth.

"I might be," she agreed softly.

They were still climbing, and Cord

glanced at his watch again.

In a few more minutes the time fuses on the thermite charges he'd planted at the Sanctuary supply huts would go off, the start of a reverberating blast which would be heard loud and clear for miles around.

When he'd got back to the Sanctuary it hadn't been difficult to talk Saat's askaris into moving their prisoners clear of the danger zone — just a hint or two that the ammunition dumps might be booby-trapped and a pointed warning that though he'd look around himself he couldn't guarantee the place would be safe.

Moyalla's army would be bitter at the loss. But the arms and ammunition back there had been enough to constitute a potential threat to peace, whoever owned them — and Field Reconnaissance made a point of not upsetting any local balance of power.

David Saat would know what had happened, but would find it hard to prove. Cord chuckled at the thought, saw Paula watching him curiously, and fished one of the cheroots from his pocket. He settled back in his seat.

"I was just thinking," he began. "In a couple of months time I'm liable to be in England, and — "

She listened, and he was satisfied.

THE END

A FOOT IN THE GRAVE
Bruce Marshall

About to be imprisoned and tortured in Buenos Aires, John Smith escapes, only to become involved in an aeroplane hijacking.

DEAD TROUBLE
Martin Carroll

Trespassing brought Jennifer Denning more than she bargained for. She was totally unprepared for the violence which was to lie in her path.

HOURS TO KILL
Ursula Curtiss

Margaret went to New Mexico to look after her sick sister's rented house and felt a sharp edge of fear when the absent landlady arrived.

THE DEATH OF ABBE DIDIER
Richard Grayson

Inspector Gautier of the Sûreté investigates three crimes which are strangely connected.

NIGHTMARE TIME
Hugh Pentecost

Have the missing major and his wife met with foul play somewhere in the Beaumont Hotel, or is their disappearance a carefully planned step in an act of treason?

BLOOD WILL OUT
Margaret Carr

Why was the manor house so oddly familiar to Elinor Howard? Who would have guessed that a Sunday School outing could lead to murder?

THE DRACULA MURDERS
Philip Daniels

The Horror Ball was interrupted by a spectral figure who warned the merrymakers they were tampering with the unknown.

THE LADIES
OF LAMBTON GREEN
Liza Shepherd

Why did murdered Robin Colquhoun's picture pose such a threat to the ladies of Lambton Green?

CARNABY
AND THE GAOLBREAKERS
Peter N. Walker

Detective Sergeant James Aloysius Carnaby-King is sent to prison as bait. When he joins in an escape he is thrown headfirst into a vicious murder hunt.

MUD IN HIS EYE
Gerald Hammond

The harbourmaster's body is found mangled beneath Major Smyle's yacht. What is the sinister significance of the illicit oysters?

THE SCAVENGERS
Bill Knox

Among the masses of struggling fish in the *Tecta's* nets was a larger, darker, ominously motionless form . . . the body of a skin diver.

DEATH IN ARCADY
Stella Phillips

Detective Inspector Matthew Furnival works unofficially with the local police when a brutal murder takes place in a caravan camp.

STORM CENTRE
Douglas Clark

Detective Chief Superintendent Masters, temporarily lecturing in a police staff college, finds there's more to the job than a few weeks relaxation in a rural setting.

THE MANUSCRIPT MURDERS
Roy Harley Lewis

Antiquarian bookseller Matthew Coll, acquires a rare 16th century manuscript. But when the Dutch professor who had discovered the journal is murdered, Coll begins to doubt its authenticity.

SHARENDEL
Margaret Carr

Ruth didn't want all that money. And she didn't want Aunt Cass to die. But at Sharendel things looked different. She began to wonder if she had a split personality.